THE UNIVERSITY CAT

A TALE FOR GROWN-UPS AND GRADUATES

JESSIKA JENVIEVE

ABOUT THE AUTHOR

Jan Sayer has worked with some incredibly exciting people who are far too celebrated to be named in her humble biography. She studied English and Drama at the legendary Bretton Hall, an experience which changed her life forever. After two years managing a bookshop, she changed direction, learned a lot of new skills and embarked on tours across Europe as both a company stage manager and a lighting designer.

For a decade, she worked as a stage manager at the Sydney Opera House, served as a producer for the Sydney 2000 Olympic Games, and most recently held the position of executive assistant at the University of Sydney.

She has written two crime thrillers, **Exposure**, set in Nova Scotia, and **We can't all die like Buddy Holly**, a UK regional crime novel.

Today she lives on the island of Texel in the Netherlands. She loves cats, sports cars and the ocean, and hopes to earn enough to feed her designer clothes habit.

She writes the **CyberCat Series** under the pen name of Jessika Jenvieve.

Sign up for the latest news at https://www.jansayer.com/

The University Cat
ISBN: 9789083325057

Copyright © 2022 by Jan Sayer
First edition: October 2014

Cover Created by BookBrush
Cat Illustrations by Andy Bridge
https://www.jansayer.com/

In memory of Mark, who loved cats

ONE

Every cat has nine lives. Penny is a super-intelligent, well-educated, Italian-speaking CyberCat with attitude. She is an elegant choc-point Siamese. She has creamy fur that gleams and delicate chocolate-brown paws. She knows that she is the cat's whiskers. She came to a sorry end in one of her previous lives, and everyone misses her. It seemed unfair that she should leave us so soon, so here are some of Penny's adventures in another life.

Penny is a very special cat with a superior education. She is largely self-taught but has, in fact, sneaked into the University with her best friend, Storm, and attended many lectures unnoticed. She sits on top of the mountain of books in the office of the Chair of English and prevents his certain death from falling books. His office is small, so the only way to store the books is up.

He is Professor Eagle, and Penny likes the way he pretends not to notice her and does not complain when he finds fur on his chair. The students often begin a sentence with, 'Hello Prof. There's a cat on ...' Then their voices drift away when they realised that two piercing blue eyes are regarding them sharply, while Penny exes an extended claw and sinks it deliberately into a collected edition of Proust.

Penny is seen and unseen; she is the very Zen of cats, and she has mastered slipping and tripping and will hiss at you in fluent Italian if she chooses.

Professor Eagle noticed her sneak in one chilly afternoon, and after attending a couple of his lectures, she followed him back to his postage-stamp-sized office and climbed the book stack. He was about to call the Head of Office Allocation, the scary Ms Matilda, but on reflection, he thought it best to say nothing.

The University's ancient halls are home to many rats and mice, although the nice white ones soon disappear behind the School of Biology's frightening Gothic-carved doors. Sometimes they emerged again, glowing frantically in the dark and make a dash for the wooded suburbs as fast as their phosphorescent paws can carry them. Why Penny should adopt Professor Eagle is a mystery lurking deep in the complexity of the cat's brain.

They both accepted each other, and on those golden afternoons when the sun poured through the courtyard windows, the Professor can be found polishing his Badge of Office with the end of his gown while Penny purrs happily.

The start of the University year is a slow process. Everyone is relaxed and tanned after their holidays, and the campus buzzes to the sound of building repairs, hedge sculpting and maintenance. The Gargoyles around the Quadrangle jut out at alarming angles, and the anxious Head of University Buildings has sleepless nights in case they should one day fall heavily onto the assembled students below. He hates the Gargoyles and thinks they are nasty, anachronistic lumps of stone. The Gargoyles have pretty much the same opinion of him. The Head of University Buildings wants to build another glass and chrome monster that will win awards. If he gets his way, the Gargoyles and their attached stone edifice will be marked for demolition very soon. The Gargoyles know they are here to stay.

Professor Eagle arrives early for another fun-filled academic day to find Penny snoozing happily on top of Yeats' Collected Works, Volumes I to IV, chosen for their soft and exquisite calf-skin binding. He nods his greeting because, officially, she is not there. If the fearsome Ms Matilda spots her, there will be trouble leading to Penny's removal if they can catch her. Professor Eagle feels she is beneficial to his research and is wondering if he could put her down as his Research Assistant. He settles down in his comfortable professorial chair and is soon dozing happily, relaxed by the gentle purrs from on top of the books.

Suddenly, a noise without, as they say in the theatrical circles. Professor Poppett's Poodle had a splendid holiday and has discovered the delights of exotic foods, such as quail and a completely unauthorised small rabbit. Beloved Poodle is allowed to accompany her owner to work during this relaxed, out of semester period. There are no unpleasant days in Puppy Day Care for the lovely Poodle, who has recently undergone a growth spurt and can now add to 'indoor barking syndrome', to a 'tendency to leap' problem.

Storm, who looks after Professor Poppett's office, has a real aversion to being leapt on by large animals and has placed a small cupboard at the side of her desk and climbs over it to gain access. So far, Beloved Poodle has remained on the other side.

Storm arrives early on Monday morning to find a small mouse caught in a trap in her office. The trap was intended for bigger rodents, and she was quite sad, as she would be happy to share her office with a little grey mouse. She tentatively approached Penny to see if she would be willing to spend a night or two in the office as a sort of deterrent. Penny gave her that 'I don't do vermin' look, but on the condition that it was merely as a preventative, she trotted along the corridor to inspect Storm's office to see if it reached the required standard for a short stay. This was a very bad moment as the black curly Poodle came bouncing around the open door, and a staring competition began. Storm had to walk around the two animals frozen in the entrance to her office. Sooner or later, Poodle will retreat, thought Storm.

An hour of mutual fascination later, and both animals turned away on some unseen cue. Poodle then bounced off to find Professor Poppett, and Penny, with a look that seemed to indicate the inferiority of Storm's office, padded her way back to the Professor Eagle's comfortable book stack.

Located close by, the University Veterinary School is an excellent place. It is full of bright people, some fearsome looking surgical instruments in a big glass case, and a three-legged dog. The instruments are marked for 'equine use only', and judging by the size, they were intended for use on a very big animal and would take at least two vets to insert if that is what you did with them. It was hard to tell. The Veterinary School is a place where everyone knows that they are doing a very good thing and they are happy in their work. What other doctor has patients with big brown eyes and adoring looks? More vets and fewer politicians would make the world a better and a more caring place.

Professor Eagle has a lovely wife. She is Dr Eagle, and she is a vet, a companion animal veterinarian, to explain the term for my American readers. She cares for your pets.

When Professor Eagle proposed marriage in his rational, business-like manner, he pointed out the marketing possibilities of a name change as a result of their formal union. A nice red rose was proffered at this juncture to add a romantic touch that he felt was needed. So, after considering economics and marketing versus sexual politics, she became Dr Eagle, and her practice then prospered, and the jokes became tolerable.

Dr Eagle came twice a week to teach and practice at the University Veterinary School and spent the other three days in her surgery at Cuddly Darlings of Darlinghurst, being studied by those big brown eyes.

She hoped Penny might one day come home to the Eyrie, their home in the Blue Mountains, but Penny watched her with suspicion when anyone mentioned 'adopt' or 'cat basket'.

Each year to raise funds for research, and allow them to treat for free the pets of less well-o owners, the Veterinary School held a Dog Show. It was open to all the dogs that regularly attended the clinic, and Beloved Poodle was one of them. The deadline for the entry form was fast approaching, and Storm had already completed one for Poodle, added some tasteful photos and delivered it in good time. Professor Poppett now attended ballet class one evening each week in training for the event. If there was some logic to this, it was not entirely clear to Storm.

A number of other high profile academic dogs would also be taking part. The Dean's bad-tempered Golden Labrador, known locally as 'the Fiend', would make his yearly appearance. The Deanery was already buzzing with staff preparing for the Fiend's bath and clip and brush, and the St John's Ambulance personnel would be standing by, as he did not take kindly to the indignity of the SudsMobile.

Mad Malcolm, the Head of University Buildings, would be entering his pug, Wrinkles, who had an agent for her TV appearances and celebrity endorsements. He expected to win lots of prizes, especially as the Fiend was sure to bite the Judges again as he had last year. He hoped that the Poodle would have an attack of leaping and be eliminated for knocking over the trophy table.

Colleagues and friends suddenly became very secretive as they started preparations for the battle ahead.

TWO

Storm arrived bright and early to find that Penny had abandoned the Professor's book stack and slept in her office for a change. She assumed that Penny had accepted the newly created role of Chief Rodent Officer. Penny's fur gleamed and glowed, and she looked in the peak of health. Storm knew that the Eagles wanted to adopt Penny. It would be a relaxed, luxurious life, but she was not sure that Penny was ready to give up her dreams of independence just yet.

Storm has a dear friend called Erickson Jon, who designs wonderful country outfits for people who never go there. There were beautiful cowboy boots in tooled leather and long leather coats for riding your horse while following your imaginary cattle trail to Halls Creek. Soft checked shirts and cute leather dog boots in case your cattle dog got wet feet crossing the Little Sandy Dessert, not to be confused with the Big Sandy Desert that took up most of the State.

Erickson was taking Storm to lunch as a special treat.

The two friends saw each other infrequently as Erickson spent his days in his studio and on faraway photo shoots.

Erickson arrived punctually in a flurry of air kisses and expensive male cologne. Curious students peeped through the glass door. Erickson looked familiar, and they assumed he was one of those TV chefs. Wasn't everyone these days?

When the greetings were over, the two smiled contently as they were old friends and could exchange 'Darhlings' with the best of them. Then Erickson saw Penny, who had been staring at him for some time, her blue eyes wide with amusement. Now I think what happened next could be described as 'a scoop up and pose with delight' movement. Erickson was so excited that he forgot the effect of cat fur on his Hugo Boss jacket, orange silk tie and designer jeans. Penny was scooped from the chair and lifted high in the air to be observed by the cameras (had there been any present).

Penny knew an opportunity when she saw one and opened her startling eyes to photoshoot size and purred ecstatically. She rolled her tail in a slinky ball and gently wrapped her paws around his wrists, adorned with golden Tiffany cuff links. It was love at first sight.

'Adorable creature,' crooned Erickson, 'is she your very own, Sweetie?'

Storm indicated that Penny was a free and independent feline who was seeking her fortune. Penny momentarily forgave Storm for assuming that she would have anything to do with Storm's rodent problem and batted her eyelashes like a lm star.

'We must have this divine creature. She must be the star of our photoshoot. Would you like to be a star, Beautiful One?'

Storm was used to fashion-world speak; otherwise, she

could have been the tiniest bit sick. She explained carefully to Erickson that Penny was free to choose her career, and as long as she was willing to go with him and he brought her back safe and sound, it would be fine.

Later that afternoon, a very shiny black Porsche arrived outside Storm's office. Penny, draped on Erickson's shoulder, where she had been during lunch nibbling on tit-bits, allowed herself to be placed on a cashmere Burberry rug on the passenger seat. After the air-kissing, Storm waved goodbye, and Penny distinctly winked at her. Professor Poppett observed the vehicle through her blinds and, thinking Erickson looked familiar, though she might mention to Storm about the health dangers of associating with celebrity chefs.

The black Porsche whooshed its way into the underground car park of Erickson Jon's design studio, famously located on the edge of the Emerald City's pristine, blue harbour. The studio was in fresh, bright colours with little scented candles and fashionable reed diffusers sprouting like weird plants from every polished surface. The natural light bounced off the walls and reflected on everyone's nicely whitened teeth.

Erickson Jon was 'A' list. He smelt 'A' list, and his clothes had little logos on them. He carried a rich smelling leather satchel. But for all this show, Erickson Jon was easily the nicest man in the city. He said thank you; he sent roses and hand-inscribed cards to his hostess after dinner, and he was kind and polite and loved by all in a city of hard souls.

Penny purred next to him. She sensed he would be very kind to her, having heard his conversation on the car phone. He ordered a special silk cushion, some fresh sardines and a pint of cream. 'Oh, and Darhling, fetch her a brush, one of those with real bristles and a little silk glove for shining her fur.'

The Porsche screeched to a halt, and Erickson leapt out athletically and opened the passenger door. Penny was lifted gently into his arms, with the rug wrapped around her to keep her warm. She looked adoringly at her new friend. When a cat looks at you ardently, those who know about the ways of cats realise that this is not quite what you think it is. Penny, special as she was, was no different from the rest. Cats seek the best advantage for themselves and simply take it. The best spot by the fire or in the sun, the best piece of fish, and the best bit of your bed. You get the affectionate look, and they get whatever they want. Adoring looks in the cat world cost nothing. Penny had her very special blue eyes and lovely fur to ensure she always got what she wanted. She just extended her little paw and wrapped you around it.

Erickson and Penny glided up in a green glass lift to the top of the building. As the double doors to Erickson Jon Designs opened as if by magic, Penny was greeted by a throng of gloriously dressed people all squealing, 'Darhling' simultaneously. There was a short delay while a spate of air-kissing took place, and finally, Penny was placed on her newly purchased cushion, and everyone stood back to admire her. Rather enjoying the attention, Penny stroked a casual paw over her perky chocolate pointed ears and contently curled her tail in an attractive shape.

Bruno, the visiting 'photo-artiste,' as his website called him, reached for his impressive camera and started snapping away, while Penny opened her big azure eyes and stared straight into the lens. She posed and preened and even batted an imaginary buttery orchestrated by a chorus of 'Coos' and 'Ahs'.

Suddenly all eyes snapped to the door of the model's dressing room, and Magnolia Potter, model of the year, owner of BeEverSoBeautiful.com, and trophy girl friend to the latest big thing in Rap and gold chains, burst in and posed herself for all to admire. Magnolia was not as tall as she said she was and was rather thinner than she ought to be. She could sense the competition four blocks away, and her heavily eye-lashed face turned slowly to Penny.

'Erickson, Sweetheart, you can't possibly mean?' she breathed, looking first at him, wide-eyed and alarmed and then at Penny as if an alley cat had peed in her hatbox. Penny looked back innocently and calmly washed her whiskers, while Magnolia pouted theatrically.

Erickson was the perfect gentleman, but he was not one to allow his ideas to be overruled, especially by his celebrity models, whose job was to be a coat hanger for his designs. He stepped forward briskly, lifted Magnolia's hand and briefly kissing her fingers then led her to his private office. His staff rushed around, making themselves scarce in a very active way. No one looked towards the heavily engraved glass window of Erickson's personal domain. Penny decided it was best to take a nap for a while.

We won't know what they said behind those closed doors. Anyone watching the shadows through the frosted glass could glimpse Magnolia's manicured hands waving a little to accompany the occasional hair tosses that she perfected doing the *Head and Shoulders* commercials that paid for her new apartment. We can be pretty sure that Erickson gently outlined his idea to Magnolia, stressing how fantastic she would look holding the 'divine little kitty'. Sneezing? No, she simply would not sneeze. Kitty had a totally aristocratic pedigree; sneezing would not occur.

A short interval of air-kissing followed, and Magnolia

swept from the office and draped herself on the leather sofa next to Penny's cushion and then simpered a little. Penny awoke, stretched and looked adoringly at Magnolia. Those who knew Penny well and had the good fortune to share her trust will have noticed the slight flicker of malice as she innocently purred at her new celebrity best friend.

THREE

Everyone was ready. The luxury bus arrived, and all the bits and bobs were loaded. Bruno and his silver camera boxes were stashed in their special area. Finally, Magnolia Potter, accompanied by her assistant and her assistant's assistant, was personally escorted to a comfortable seat at the front by Erickson himself. As Erickson wrapped the designer rug over Magnolia's bony knees, she looked around deliberately and enquired,

'But where is the Sweet One? Where is Darhling Penny?'

This was a clever ploy to make sure she kept Penny in her sights at all times. Several emphatic head tosses and hair flicks followed. Erickson said that Penny would be travelling with him. There was just a tiny, tiny flicker of a heavily botoxed brow as Magnolia registered her annoyance at the cat going in the Porsche while she was on the bus with the luggage. Erickson, always the master of difficult moments, did a little fingertip kissing to buy time and then reassured Magnolia.

'My Darhling, Penny might be alarmed, might put out a

little paw to steady herself around the corners, she might fall, and I know you would be so, so devastated if the beautiful kitty was even a tiny bit frightened, you with your wonderful, gentle, loving nature. I know how devoted you are to animals.'

Magnolia's very sad handbag-sized lapdog, left to pine alone in Los Angeles, would have an opinion about this.

'I shall take Penny in the car because I know how much you adore her,' said Erickson, firmly closing the discussion.

It was a miracle that no one laughed. So Magnolia, her ego soothed, settled down for the drive to the photo-shoot location, and Erickson took Penny for a quick cream-topped babycino in his favourite cafe.

The shoot was to be at the Stables. Magnolia would be wearing many very sporty riding outfits, holding Erickson's gorgeous leather bags, and wearing his fashionable boots. A horse was hired for the day. Penny, who colour-toned perfectly with the soft creamy brown leather, would be shown peeping out of the bags or sitting brightly on the saddle. The horse had not been consulted about this, but Erickson was confident that after a morning with Magnolia, the horse would agree to anything to get her off his back.

The stylist hovered around Magnolia, brushing and flicking. The groom led out the horse, now known as 'The Horse', and as he handed the lavish leather reins to Magnolia, she wrinkled her nose as if a nasty smell might be passing. Finally, Penny was placed on the saddle, and a fluffy mouse on a stick was waved to show her which way to look. Penny looked beautiful; the assistants had brushed her and petted her, and she certainly didn't need a toy mouse to tell her to look straight at the camera. Penny set her great big eyes to intense, and the Horse, sensing this might be his big chance too, uttered his lashes in a very becoming manner.

Magnolia, feeling that she might be out-shone, turned on her full camera-ready glare, and Bruno chatted away encouragingly as his camera clicked.

'Smoulder, that's it and the Big Smile, that's it, give it to me. Stupendo, Bellissimo, so Beautiful. Now Bright Eyes, wider, brighter, come on, simmer for me.'

The next shot was to feature the overnight bags. A warm leather-scented arrangement of butter-soft bags was placed on a sort of equestrian-looking construction of straw bales with a few bits of horse paraphernalia. The Horse was led to stand behind this artistic creation and with a carrot was encouraged to look towards the bags. Penny was in the open satchel and arranged with care, so her wonderful chocolate paws draped over the edge. While all this was happening in her dressing room, a rather stroppy Magnolia was rude to her hairdresser, whose fault it was for her bad hair day.

All eyes swivelled to the open door as she stomped out, swishing a riding crop. She looked steadily at the display and snapped.

'And where am I supposed to stand? Surely not to one side. Where's Erickson?'

A cat and a horse were upstaging Magnolia for the first time in her life.

Erickson arrived promptly, and Magnolia was led firmly outside to be soothed and calmed. Not wanting to miss the chance of a brilliant shot, Bruno snapped away at Penny and the Horse, who both rose splendidly to the occasion. Eventually, Magnolia was led back, dabbing at her eyes with a tissue. Everyone knew that Erickson had finally used his ultimate weapon, the suggestion of a younger model, hungry for the opportunity and whom he might reluctantly have to use if his 'Darhling Magnolia' deserted him.

Magnolia stood patting the Horse's muzzle and tried to look as if she was enjoying her day. Penny and the Horse were undoubtedly enjoying theirs. It was forty or so minutes later, after a number of arranged poses, Bruno declared he was happy, and it was 'in the can'. Magnolia defeated and resumed her sulky face while Penny leapt from the bag into Erickson's arms to be stroked and praised.

It was just as Magnolia revolved on her killer heels that a loud 'plop' sounded behind her. The Horse, in his delight, had signalled his enjoyable day in the most-horsey way possible. There was a squawk from Magnolia as she turned to dash away from the rich, stable smell that was wafting towards her.

It is important to note here that most models cannot walk more than a few straight-line steps in stilettos. Turns are infrequent and choreographed. And Magnolia, to give her a little credit, had been standing for some time in the equestrian version of killer-heels. Screwing up her nose and turning to run to her scented dressing room, she mismanaged her turn and was next seen face down in the straw.

There was a sudden heavy hush, followed by another joyous 'plop' from the Horse. Everyone strained not to laugh as Magnolia, liberally decorated with straw, was lifted by her assistants and carried to her dressing room in a sort of stage faint. The door slammed.

Everyone spontaneously broke into fits of laughter.

THAT NIGHT there was to be a grand supper party at a posh restaurant set over the sparkling blue sea at a very famous beach. Erickson needed a nap after his exhausting day with the awful Magnolia. Bruno sent him some of the photographs, and he was afraid to admit that those featuring

Penny and the Horse looked so much better without the sulky model's pout. He would wait until she was back with her celebrity rapper in LA and then discreetly tell her agent. One shot of her frozen smile would be quite enough, and her contract did not explicitly state how many photographs of her must be used. He could almost hear the hysterical screams echoing across the Pacific. Erickson headed for his luxury king-size bed with gold silk sheets, and attired only in a designer T-shirt and cute shorts, stretched out for a few hours' sleep. I am shocked to say that Penny went with him.

Meanwhile, in the thousand-dollar-a-night hotel overlooking the Opera House, Magnolia was rude to her assistant, her assistant's assistant and her hairdresser while her bath was drawn. A rail of complimentary designer gowns was wheeled in with a flourish, and the arduous task of choosing an evening dress began.

The assistant was reading out the guest list, and her assistant was calling up the other celebrity assistants to check that no one would dare to wear the same outfit. All waited in anticipation. Once a gown was selected, all could proceed down the merry road of shoes, jewels, bag, and gloves – do we need gloves? The stylist could then choose the lingerie to pull in the wobbly bits and plumb out the little bony bits that might have suddenly appeared on the supermodel's skeletal frame.

Then with all the fanfare of an Oscar announcement, a dress was chosen, and Magnolia stomped to her bath, facial and massage, while everyone else had a cup of tea and a biscuit. The chosen gown was white and tight with a delicate smattering of sequins at the fishtail hem. Something very tight and smoothing would be worn underneath, and super high-heeled silver sandals would finish off the ensemble. The stylist arranged a small feathery headpiece and a pile of silver cuffs to complete the look. Magnolia would make her farewell entrance as a feast of summer beauty, like a silver mermaid silhouetted by the ocean, and everyone else would get a night's sleep at last.

Erickson and Penny awoke and dined together on a plate of sushi and a small glass/ dish of milk. Penny was gently brushed, given a diamanté collar to wear and, escorted by Erickson in a beautiful white tuxedo jacket, she climbed onto her cushion in the Porsche, and they glided off to the supper party.

It was a warm, calm night, and the restaurant glowed with little candles in dishes while plates of sushi and fruits were handed round by dark-eyed staff, bronzed, buffed and gleaming, just in case anyone noticed them. Magnolia was fashionably late, having complained loudly in the limousine that her feet hurt. She swooped into the restaurant while media-pack cameras flashed, and Erickson kissed her hand ostentatiously. She was handed a crystal ute of champagne, and as eating was completely out of the question, she waved a dismissive hand at the waiters rather than giving them a polite 'no, thank you'.

The media took notes, and everyone else snapped their selfies. Erickson made a charming speech thanking Magnolia for being the delight of the photo-shoot and praising her beauty and grace. Everyone else stifled a laugh and sincerely hoped she would never leave Los Angeles again.

And finally, it was time to go. A huge chocolate gâteau, heavily attacked by the hungry guests, was earlier placed on a table towards the entrance. It had been a triumph, and the chef was delighted by its popularity and devastated that it had been eaten. Penny had developed a taste for the creamy decoration. While all eyes were on Magnolia, she leapt gracefully onto the table and finished off the creamy curls at the edge of this masterpiece of pâtisserie.

Penny watched Magnolia as she swivelled on her heels before making her exit. This movement was done slowly, so the assembled press could get their cameras ready for the departing shot of the ever-so tight white gown and the sheen of her fake suntanned back. Erickson took her hand and readied himself to escort her to the limousine before returning for a long-awaited beer.

They slowly walked to the door, and seconds before Magnolia turned to flash her peroxide white teeth at the cameras, Penny gently placed her chocolate-coated delicate chocolate paw on the luscious curve of Magnolia's derrière. Magnolia smiled without noticing Penny and turned for the door. There, to the delight of the assembled media, at the back of the pure white gown was a perfect paw print in the middle of her pert bottom. The cameras flashed frantically, and within seconds, the tweets went worldwide. Penny posed by the cake and meticulously cleaned her paws while maintaining an air of complete innocence.

The rest of the evening was a joyous celebration by the happy, hard-working people finally free of the vile Magnolia. Erickson had a glass of beer, and Penny ate the rest of the cream cake. A sleepy Penny was transported lovingly for another night in Erickson's luxury apartment.

The next morning, Storm arrived to find Penny fast asleep on a silk cushion outside her office. Placed under the cushion was a small blue box containing a little Tiffany trinket. The two friends were reunited with a warm hug, and Penny slinked o for the comfortable book stack in Professor Eagle's office and a couple of days of contented purring after her adventure.

. . .

FOUR

Sometimes Penny needed a change. She had received lots of tasty treats, and because of her recent rich, luxurious diet, a few essential items of plain food were required to give balance. Penny fancied a mouse. A delicious, crunchy meal with all the added benefits of a lot of healthy exercise. Mousing was a precise, aerobic activity. Ah, the anticipation! After she spent several days catching up on her catnaps, and it was time to slide silently o the book stack and slink out unnoticed at twilight.

University mice come in two types, escaped and local. The escaped sort are white and sometimes they glow in the dark. These can be toyed with but never ever eaten. The locals are brown and fast and have learned to live above ground lest they become the subject of notice. Sometimes they are grey if they live that long.

The old buildings have very complex roofs with gullies and gutters. In the oldest part of the Quadrangle, the blue slate roofs have a system of valleys, waterspouts and drainpipes to remove the water from the building's vicinity via the overhanging eaves.

Most remarkable of all are the Gargoyles, a type of stone waterspout carved in the form of a mythical beast with a spout that diverts the water away from the walls. The name comes from the French word *gargouille*, meaning gullet in English. I expect they are starting to sound unattractive already.

In this forest of architectural wonders, the mice and their larger cousins, both the marsupial and the un-pocketed kind, scamper happily among the roosting bats. No students up here to squeal horribly at the sight of a tiny, harmless mouse. The drainpipes are fat, ornate and easy to climb, and convenient attic windows lead to warm rooms for further rest and recuperation.

A few weeks of reconnaissance had revealed this twilight world of delicious opportunities, and Penny felt it was time to venture inside. She simply strolled unnoticed to the top floor to save effort, and finding an open attic window, stepped lightly onto the roof. Set into the Great Big Hall's slate roof were small openings filled with dark blue glass that filtered a mysterious light into the vast hall.

This part of the roof had a splendid deep gulley to walk along and observe the tiled Museum roof just below. Penny finally selected a comfortable space in the guttering to begin her silent observation of the available foodstuffs. As the sun set, she stretched out and watched while waiting for the set menu to arrive.

The master masons who built the University had a good sense of humour and when instructed to provide the standard gargoyle for water drainage, they got over-excited and embellished the building with a whole lot of non-practical cravings called Grotesques. It is a common belief that these wonderful stone bestiaries are also called Gargoyles. They are said to frighten off harmful spirits and protect the buildings they guard. They nicely embodied the concept of evil, sending a stark message to students and evil spirits alike. These vast stone creatures did not care what you called them, and those approaching the Gothic splendour at night were advised to use caution.

The craftsmen, not having much supervision in the early years of construction and having got a remit to embellish, spotted the chance for a lifetime's creative work, well paid and steady, and so went ahead and filled every available space with a unique beast. As magically happens, if you are a stone beast that is not fixed down by a waterspout, your exact location can become fluid. The Gargoyles could and did move! But only if you were not watching them. There were suspicions, of course.

Old and venerable members of the Senate were sure that the beast with the pointy beak and arched wings had been in one place on Monday and by Wednesday had relocated to another. This confusion was attributed to intensive research activities and too many pedagogical encounters. Those who think that the Gargoyles are simply made of stone are terribly mistaken. The Gargoyles had arranged themselves into academic faculties as did their human counterparts, and as in all educational institutions, regular meetings were required to talk endlessly and decide even less.

Penny watched without moving a whisker as the Gargoyles of the Faculty of Arts, Rhetoric and Thematic Studies (F.A.R.T. S) assembled a few meters below her on the Museum rooftop for their weekly meeting. Her sharp eyes first picked out their outlines in the twilight as the huge shapes soared against the reddening sky.

An observer looking up might have thought that an eye test was in order, and as it was impossible to mistake them for regular birds, the observer was left wondering why eagles were flying over the dreaming spires. There were strange calls very far beyond the range of human hearing. The whales out at sea heard them and splashed away contemptuously. Their species was far older and so much wiser. Smaller creatures simply ran for cover.

Gargoyois is not a language as we understand it; it is a set of descriptive sounds joined together, phonetics if you like. Pioneering linguists have not advanced much in this area of study, and those who have undertaken eld research do not speak of it or had never been found alive or sane. Gargoyles have all the time in the world and are confident they will be there for eternity, so there is no need for a complex set of semantics and pragmatics just yet. For them, language was created to be as annoying as possible to other Gargoyles. It is very direct. They are well aware of the quantity of human gobbledygook going on below them and felt no need to develop any obscure or esoteric semiotics just yet. Gargoyles have a dark vocabulary.

A particularly attractive red sunset was now washing across the city below. Obscenely noisy birds were pushing each other out of trees as they got bedded down for the night. The spider had eaten her last mosquito and was rolling up into her leaf home and sealing the door. Penny felt a cold breeze pass through her fur, and she sunk lower behind the stone parapet, judging correctly that being visible was not a good plan. As usual, Penny's feline instincts were quite right. She may be in search of a fat, succulent mouse, but below her were assembling a group of monsters that looked as if they might eat anything they fancied. Indeed, the Gargoyles were carnivorous, and some were surprisingly quick.

FIVE

It is not often that one of those cute, cuddly Golden Labradors so loved by toilet tissue manufacturers manages to grow up into a snarling, salivating monster. The Dean's bad-tempered Golden Labrador, commonly known as the Fiend, was a freak of nature. It snarled and snapped and still looked a picture of canine cuteness until your hand was in close range. The Deanery staff had a sliding scale of payments for any injuries suffered, and although actual bodily harm was usually avoided, damage to stockings, trousers, and chewed handbags was common. It is thought that the Dean lectured to the poor creature in Latin when it first arrived puppy-perfect to delight his family, and the sound of his voice still has horrible consequences to this day.

A number of tactics were craftily employed to allow the Fiend to participate in the Dog Show, including an embroidered muzzle made by Mrs Dean, the blonde former actress. The latter graced the Dean's dining table and spoke with a suspicious southern American accent but insisted she was Canadian.

The Head of University Buildings, who was known locally as Mad Malcolm, would be entering his pug, Wrinkles, on the recommendation of the agent employed to ensure that Wrinkles made an income stream that exceeded the cost of dog food and vet bills. Wrinkles also featured heavily in promoting toilet tissue and received a four-figure sum for one day's rolling around on a pink mat wrapped in pink tissue. Wrinkles would soon be the owner of an excellent new BMW to be chauffeured by Mad Malcolm on her behalf. The tax advantages of this arrangement were very elegantly contrived.

As Professor Poppett's Poodle was a newcomer to the yearly show and still relatively a puppy, the two old hands contrived to accidentally bump into each other next to the Mummy of Horus, which allowed them to hatch a cunning plan unobserved in the shadow of the giant sarcophagus.

'It won't win, you know,' observed the Dean out of thin air, for the conversation had not officially begun.

Both men were trying and failing to look inconspicuous among the antiquities and crowds of Chinese tourists.

'I know,' hissed Mad Malcolm, 'but just in case, we should have a plan.'

'I don't see why,' snapped The Dean, not used to be being contradicted.

A silent sulk took place.

'All I am suggesting,' whispered Mad Malcolm urgently, 'was in the event of the Poodle seeming to have the advantage, some slight action might occur. A little distraction from without, as they say in theatrical circles.'

Malcolm had never been in a theatrical circle in his life and was unlikely to be invited to join one. The Dean, on the other hand, observed theatrical tantrums at his dining table regularly on account of his wife blaming him for her failure to obtain the lead role in the latest musical. Her ability to sing in tune was questionable.

A sudden flush of snap-happy tourists obliged the two to wander around pretending to be scholarly. The Dean looked at the Roman pottery. Mad Malcolm studied the wood beetles in the Museum's historic panelling and longed for a wrecking ball to obliterate neo-Gothic architecture from his world.

Coming together again near the Etruscan urns, the Dean demanded to know what 'slight action' might occur. Mad Malcolm had not given this much thought as yet, but he favoured a loud noise to alarm and make Poodle go out of control. As the Dog Show was to be held on the hallowed lawns of the Quadrangle for the first time, he suggested that the placing of a motor vehicle close by would be possible. He hinted that his new BMW might be available for such a mission.

'Some sort of horn, you mean?' insisted the Dean, who still drove his ancient Ford to annoy his wife.

'And the Poodle would go wild and out of control and be disqualified,' explained Malcolm.

'The Fiend might also, 'go wild,' as you put it.' The Dean was a lateral thinker and philosopher.

'But we know when the noise will occur,' said Mad Malcolm confidently.

'The dogs won't,' snapped the Dean.

A party of high school students looking for nude statues arrived and forced the sub-committee apart, and so both men sidled to the exits.

Emails would be exchanged later.

SIX

**Minutes of the Meeting of Monday 12 May 2014
The Board Room, 3-4pm
Attendees: Professor Fang (Chair), Dr Eagle, Ms
Von Katten (Community Representative).
Also in attendance: Mr Thickett (Head
Groundsman), Ms Gloriana Groom (SudsMo-
bile), and Mr Fred Planet (Event Coordinator).**

1. Minutes of the Meeting of 14 October 2013.
The minutes of Monday 14 October 2013 were accepted as
an accurate record.
2. Matters Arising: None.
3. Dog Show 2014.

Professor Fang welcomed Mr Thickett and Mr
Fred Planet to the meeting to discuss the Dog Show for
2014. He outlined the new and special circumstances of the
2014 event, which was to be held on the Quadrangle lawn
for the first time. He briefly introduced the guests, outlined
their special skills and how they would contribute to making

the event successful and memorable while protecting the heritage aspects of the University site, namely the lawn.

He noted that the lawn in question was almost ten years old and was kept in pristine condition by the extraordinary efforts of Mr Thickett's team and a grant from the state government for special lawn food and a watering permit.

Mr Planet outlined the plans for protecting the lawn whilst ensuring the safety of the public and competitors. The public would be seated around three sides on fixed seating placed on special trestles that would each have four minor points of impact on the lawn. These areas of turf would be removed and replaced after the event. The audience exits and entrances would be along the paved areas at the centre and on each side. This would minimise the number of persons actually walking on the lawn itself.

The judge's podium would be on the opposite side to the audience on the paved area. The dogs and handlers would arrive and leave via the Museum side of the Quadrangle, and the dog marshalling area would be in the covered, paved arcade directly outside the Museum, which would be closed during the event. Ms Gloriana Groom from SudsMobile would have a special grooming area here with a generous hot water supply from the cleaning cupboard.

The meeting agreed that this was an excellent plan.

Mr Thickett, then, expressed his concern about 'little accidents'. He noted that the dogs were to be marshalled on the paved area, which could be cleaned in the event of a mishap but suppose there was a mishap on THE LAWN. Mr Thickett said that he had no direct experience of dogs or dog shows.

Ms Von Katten, representing the community, assured Mr Thickett that there was seldom a mishap whilst the dogs were parading. These were highly trained animals, with responsible owners who would ensure that any small items of used food would be quickly retrieved, sealed in a biodegradable plastic bag and placed in the receptacles that would be provided in the marshalling area. Show dogs, she advised the meeting, were never fed before the event. The marshals would be provided with the very latest 'pooper-scoopers' in a variety of biodegradable plastics.

Mr Thickett thanked Ms Von Katten and the committee for their concern about HIS LAWN.

The meeting then discussed the catering at length.

SEVEN

It is time to return to Penny and consider her
tricky situation. Let's look down from Penny's parapet and
watch the arrivals on the Museum roof directly below her.

First, the sun set, and all around were sinister black
shadows. The places between the shadows, the deepest
darkest spots, are where you must look carefully for danger.
Ensure that your tail is coiled up in case of an involuntary
twitch, you betray your hiding place. Tuck tightly beneath
you your delicate chocolate paws. And don't overthink the
piles of weathered bones strewn over the tiles. These are
ancient bones, and maybe those are teeth marks or claw
marks. Penny realised that some of those yellowing skele-
tons were suspiciously large and not her idea of a juicy
mouse supper. She sank lower and watched appre-
hensively.

A bit of Gargoyle evolution is required at this point.
Gargoyles are made of stone. In this case, it is sandstone,
which is also known as yellow stone. Now, this is where
evolution kicks in. Sedimentary rocks were laid down on the
Earth's surface, primarily underwater in layers or strata.

Depending on their geological makeup, these sedimentary rocks may preserve previous life-forms and signs of surface activity, like fossils, tracks, ripple marks and so on.

So, millions and millions and millions of years ago, this lovely buttery yellow stone was formed, and deep inside is sand and shells and lots of juicy sea creatures and organisms like krill, the stuff that whales eat. Sandstone is made of things that were alive and, strangely, might still be alive. Now you understand why those enormous stone carvings, officially regarded as inanimate, can come to life again at any time. When it suits them, of course, and when no one is watching. Twilight is best; that's the time when your eyes play the most tricks.

So now you are wondering about the bones. Gargoyles were not officially designed to eat food. But they do, and they kill, for pleasure. It is the worst sort of killing when nothing is spared just because it's fun. And they are immortal, so they don't care. Penny was right to hide in the shadows because if they see her, they will kill her.

For fun.

There is a sound of huge damp wings, followed by a smack on the tiles as the first Gargoyle landed heavily. His name was Fishbeak. Gargoyle names come from their design drawings, so they have the title that their creator gave them as they grew slowly from the dark recesses of his imagination and found their way onto the building's blueprints.

Fishbeak was in a foul mood. If he could speak, he would have told you just how foul his mood was, but he was inconveniently created with a fish in his mouth, so his communications were limited to staring, glaring, and a series of shy snorts. His moods often reduced him to violently tearing his victims into small pieces with his eight huge claws and stamping on them in a rage.

His belly had an armoured layer of scales like those on his pointy beak. His wings rested close to his back in a carapace covered in bony skin. These were not like the soft geometric scales of a fish but like the hard scales of a crocodile, the largest and most aggressive of reptiles. His squat, strong legs helped to keep him from falling sideways due to the weight of his wings or forwards due to the weight of the large fish in his mouth. Keeping upright was a constant effort.

He was always the first to arrive, as he was not off chatting somewhere. With his impressive size and ability for strong, decisive action, he elected the Chair of the Gargoyle Committee, which was about to convene. To ensure the rest of the members' attendance, he had brought along a selection of recently dead rats that he now released from his bloodstained claws with a sickening squelch as they landed on the tiles.

Next to arrive was Dragonclaw. He slithered heavily up the drainpipe from the lower turret with his long tail working hard to balance his weight. He was a tight bundle of sinew and muscle, strength and malice. His ever-open mouth displayed a terrifying row of teeth with which he liked to tear his prey. He was carved with the mane of a lion containing some very effeminate curls. The two boar tusks on his snout nicely balanced the curly mane. The shy end of the long, heavy tail had a distinctly mermaidy look to it, which he loathed. He also had a terrible lisp and, over the centuries, had developed the annoying habit of describing his actions in case anyone was in doubt of what he was doing.

He studied Fishbeak and the pile of dark, smelly fur that lay at his feet.

'ohh tanks yus for dems wrodents wuns ups to him ans collectinked dems.'

He then retreated to a safe distance.

'chews ons his wrodents: mmmmm.'

Fishbeak regarded him with a look of total disdain and then watched enviously as his colleague ate. Gargoyles keep a respectful distance from one another, especially when the critical business of chewing is in progress.

There was a rushing of wings and scraping claws, and next to arrive was Dogface. His creator had a Great Dane, of which he was very fond, despite its ugliness. So, his carving had taken on the look of his pet, with curly whiskers, impressive canines and a tendency to drool.

Dogface had the usual eight claws and short, fat wings like a bat. From there, backwards, he was a fish with scales, and a shark-fin tipped tail. It took him a few moments to fold his fat wings to allow movement, and he too wandered over to get his share of the rats. He looked toward his companions, and after getting a snort from Fishbeak, he inquired as to the health of Dragonclaw.

'I doin goods tanks yus; I evens gotted sums wrodents tonights hehehe.'

The other Gargoyles rolled their eyes, and assuming that no further pleasantries were to be observed, Dogface collected his share of the rats and got to work with his claws. The three resembled a particularly macabre cooking class.

Penny kept as still as a hunting leopard. She watched and waited, for it was too late to leave, and she was unsure of just how fast these monsters might move. She was quick, but they had wings.

Fishbeak stamped his feet on the roof, indicating that the meeting was in order, and the others turned their bloodstained faces to him. He snorted to Dogface to propose the motion.

'I move that this meeting come to order and consider the as-yet un-investigated resources that lay below us inside the Museum. I have undertaken an examination of the area in question and found that it contains several deceased persons and animals preserved in a nutritious substance. These are wrapped in a formal covering of linen, which can be easily removed, and at present, the stone lids of the receptacles containing these exhibits are conveniently open. I focused my initial examination on a small item that used to be of a type of feline. It proved very chewy, and I managed to detach one of the toes. My proposal to this meeting is that a further investigation is carried out on the evening of the Dog Show when attention is elsewhere, and we will be undisturbed.'

The other Gargoyles tapped their claws in approval, and Penny shuddered. An extended period of silence followed as the Gargoyles continued to tear the remains of the rats into small pieces. She wondered if they could smell her, or sense her, or even if their vision was supernatural and allowed them to look through the stone. Penny was cold and very afraid.

Now let's go back a little to view these events through the three Gargoyles' collective and individual thoughts. We have watched the scene from Penny's perspective, and in the interest of total fairness to all species and the light of scientific study, we should look at this scene from the Gargoyle's point of view.

Gargoyles are not obliged to use speech and can share their thoughts collectively and separately. Some liked to talk out loud, which can be annoying and confusing and very noisy, and Dragonclaw preferred the excellent sound of his own voice and the extraordinary range of grunts and snorts that he could generate with a stone throat. Those, like Dogface, imitated the posh pearly sounds of the University academics. Some, like poor Fishbeak, just have to put up with a fish permanently stuck in their mouth.

These events as seen in the Gargoyle's collective thoughts. Fishbeak landed heavily in his usual foul mood. The committee was about to convene. The rest of the members had not arrived, and he was clutching a pile of dead rats, which he was unable to nibble into satisfyingly bloody pieces. He cursed his creator. He had an uncomfortable feeling he was being watched, and from the corner of his bulging eyes, he could just make out a faint outline of a quivering furry body tucked behind the parapet above him. Too small to be a threat, and yet, big enough to torture when captured later. He sniffed and detected a feline odour with a distinct hint of advanced cunning.

Later, he thought, later, if the other buffoons don't spot it, it will be mine to play with. He could almost feel the little creature trembling between his claws. He heard the sounds of Dragonclaw slithering heavily up the drainpipe from the lower turret with his long tail working hard to balance up his weight. Overweight, thought Fishbeak, a fundamentally unbalanced design, all mouth and no posterior. He did have a strong desire to have the same set of impressive sinews and muscles and some of Dragonclaw's strength.

Dragonclaw arrived and displayed his terrifying row of teeth with a gust of foul breath thrown in. He studied Fishbeak and the pile of dark, smelly fur that lay on the roof tiles at his feet. He gave the tiles an exploratory tap with his claws and lisped out loud, as he knew it was annoying.

'I cwacked ves tiles in wuns nighted justs scrwinked dems to sees hows manys yus cans cracks hehehehe.'

Fishbeak snorted and had some private thoughts about Dragonclaw being too close to the ground and mixing too freely with the students. Not a good thing, in Fishbeak's opinion. He kept a respectful distance while his colleague was chewing away at his rat. Dragonclaw emitted too many overpowering smells of his own to notice the faint feline smell wafting down from the parapet. He did get a strong sense there was an observer and marked the intruder down for a little dismemberment later that evening if his colleagues did not spot it.

A rushing of wings and scraping claws announced the arrival of Dogface. Damn wings, he muttered as he always did when obliged to fold them to allow movement on the ground and then he wandered over to get his share of the rats. After he had received the usual snort from Fishbeak, to be particularly irritating, he inquired about the health of Dragonclaw, as he knew he would get the usual lisp and simper.

'I doin goods tanks yus; I evens gotted sums wrodents tonights hehehe.'

Everyone rolled their eyes while Dogface collected his share of the rats and took his place, and got to work with his claws. The three were aware of the small presence pressed close behind the parapet and were considering the possibility of future pleasing entertainment. Whatever it was, and it might be quick, but they had the advantage of wings.

Fishbeak had quite enough of watching the others chew their rats and stamped his foot on the roof to call the meeting to order. Bloodstained faces turned to him as he snorted to Dogface to propose the motion.

There was a respectful silence while the motion was

proposed, and then the chewing continued. Then it was time to approve the motion in the usual manner, and all three tapped their claws on the tiles. In the following silence, as they tore into the rats, as they could smell and sense the strange presence cowering behind the stone parapet.

Each had the same thought. Whatever it was, it would be cold and very, very afraid.

EIGHT

Professor Eagle arrived the next morning and looked around for Penny. She had returned from her last trip, looking plump and happy and smelling faintly of perfume and chocolate. After a few days of sleep and grooming, she disappeared one evening and had not returned. His wife, Dr Eagle, who was well-versed in the habits of cats, said she was off hunting and prowling, and she was pretty safe within the University grounds. Professor Eagle looked longingly at the dent in his book stack's top book where she usually lay and felt dreadfully sad and lonely. Penny was his muse, and he missed her gentle purr while he worked.

Unable to relax, he wandered a few doors down to Storm's office to ask for news. Storm shook her head forlornly and handed him an impressive cream envelope that had arrived in the mail. Professors get lots of big envelopes, usually inviting them to attend very pompous events and asking them to pay for their dinner. This big cream envelope contained a formal invitation to be the Guest Judge at the forthcoming Dog Show. He was delighted, as he knew his wife was invited as the official veterinarian to deal with any attacks of pet nerves.

The Chair of the Judges' was to be Professor Fang, the President of the Canine Dentistry Association, and the community representative was Ms Von Katten, a local pet owner. He replied right away and later received a hand-delivered, glossy information pack from Fred Planet, the event coordinator.

News of his appointment to the Judges' Panel spread like wildfire, and several unexpected invitations to attend other events started to arrive. Professor Eagle had suddenly been added to everyone's guest list. He received an invitation from the Head of University Buildings to attend a cream tea to celebrate a new lift installed in the library.

The Dean personally asked him to speak at a Graduation Ceremony later that year. A couple of requests to comment to the media on obscure literary topics arrived via Professor Poppett's office. He expected that he had simply been added to these lists due to his academic endeavours.

Professor Poppett's poodle arrived unexpectedly one afternoon at his office's open door, looking groomed and woolly, and executed some formal obedience exercises. The fact that all the invites came from dog owners was something he did not consider relevant, as he was delighted that he was at last recognised for his work in obscure literary studies.

Another day passed and still Penny had not returned. Professor Eagle decided it was time for action, but as he could not go around asking about a cat that was not supposed to be there, it made for a delicate situation. He decided to take a literary approach, and his students suddenly were asked to write a short descriptive essay or poem about an animal they had observed in the University.

The assignment outline was intriguing, using the words' feline' and 'ailurophile' on numerous occasions. There was even 'chatoyant' as a descriptive suggestion. There were many animals in the University's grounds, including the three-legged dog in the Veterinary School and the army of strangely glowing mice in Nuclear Physics. The School of Chemistry also had a couple of pink mice who could not be explained by any particular experiment but ate a lot and were very happy on their little wheel. There were flocks of cockatoos nesting in the trees and possums wandering around the sports oval. Most were beyond the control of any particular Faculty.

The students presented their work at the next day's tutorial. Professor Eagle looked glum, and all his students tried very hard to cheer him up. After sitting through two different and very long, *Odes to a Lonely Possum*, and a vivid descriptive essay about happy mice mating in the Students' Union basement, the Professor concluded that Penny was nowhere to be seen and sadly went home to a shepherd's pie.

NINE

Ms Gloriana Groom had a Master's Degree in Business Studies. She was a pert, pretty woman of the fatally pink kind. Her working uniform was adorned with pink bows on tiny poodles. She wore a bow in her hair and had a mind as sharp as a razor. She decided early on that the fabulous academic qualifications would only help if she carved her way into the business world, so she set about building her empire.

She made a list of the practical skills required. She had excellent accounting skills, a list of contacts of the rich and silly kind and a firm way of making sure she was always paid and on time. She was also pretty, very articulate and looked fantastic with a big pink bow perched on top of her head. She could pin you to the wall with a slight lift of one shapely eyebrow. Ms Groom had a fearsome Chinese grandmother whose empire had once stretched from Peking to Hong Kong, and Ms Groom had inherited her ancestor's steely exterior and probably her ability to run an opium den.

So SudsMobile was created, and the pretty pink bows

adorned the specially designed mobile dog-washing salon, which was pulled along by a cute pink 4WD, which had the o-road capacity of a goldfish. Ms Groom was almost ready to start her franchises after appearing on all the Good Morning and Drive Time shows on radio and TV. She was also featured each week in the local papers, as it was impossible to miss the SudsMobile wagon parked strategically at every community event. It made an excellent background for photographs.

Ms Groom's list of contacts included all the University pet owners. She even allowed the Dean to bring the Fiend to her salon provided a strong muzzle was attached first. Ms Groom invested in some long rubber gloves of the dominatrix type for this particular client. She was very thrilled to be invited to join the planning committee for the annual Dog Show. This was brilliant publicity, ensuring the SudsMobile Salon was in a prominent place for all to see, and it also allowed her to build up her client list. Ms Groom intended to franchise nationally and be the CEO of a worldwide company before she was thirty-five. Her website groaned under the bows and cute client photos and words of praise. It was positively infested with 'likes'.

Ms Groom did have a dark secret. This was a well-kept secret, as Gloriana Groom adored and worshipped cats. The big problem was that they did not take to the SudsMobile as well as dogs, which were fundamentally stupid creatures. She washed her cats in a sunken bath in her home, installed with them in mind, and her four sleek Siamese cats (two seal points and two lilac points) happily spread their fur across every corner of her little house. Had this secret been exposed, her credibility as the kind, gentle groom to superior dogs would have taken a bit of a dent.

Ms Groom was tough, fearless and would probably

spike the drinks of her competitors if required. The resemblance to her ancestor was not just physical with her jet-black hair and elegant figure; she too possessed her grandmother's ability to walk firmly over all who stood in her way.

Her clients thought her amazing. Her service, her care and attention to their pets was excellent if a little pricey. But you got what you paid for, and your dog emerged from the suds smelling of roses and you were saved the trouble of bathing it yourself. They simply could not work out the feeling of anxiety that washed over them when Ms Groom's beautiful figure in a cute pink uniform arrived at their home. They handed over the money and their pet and retreated indoors until the job was done. Ms Groom was likely to make a million dollars without much difficulty and very soon, too.

TEN

DR ROBERT PARKER-BETTS WAS NOT SIX-FOOT-TALL. This unfortunate fact had ruled his life, despite his being way above average intelligence. He lived with his parents in the spare garage of their enormous house that sprawled down the suburban hillside.

They were very nice, crazy people, but he sometimes wished he had been adopted. The family glue had not quite stuck, and they all lived separate lives and were polite to each other as required. His mother spent her life sitting on the sofa arguing with the TV, surrounded by great piles of hissing fur. It was sometimes hard to see exactly how many cats there were as their tails merged to create a giant rug that trailed over the edge of the furniture. His father did something scientific, which involved trips to remote salt flats and very long walks to keep him fit and hearty.

The adolescent Dr Robert Parker-Betts saw a film one day and decided to become an archaeologist. He applied his mind to the task and was successful, as his family always were, as they did not have to worry much about who paid for the food. Regrettably, no amount of generous trust funds could alter the fact that Dr Robert Parker-Betts was not six-foot-tall, and he wanted so very much to be like his hero. He was fit and active, as was required by a profession that involved a lot of digging.

After recoiling in horror at the costume required for modern cycling, he bought a vintage motorbike, just like his hero, and settled down happily to work in the University Museum. He was a good companion and was very well-liked by his trivia night pals and his colleagues, but somehow no one wanted to marry him. He converted the spare garage into a comfortable studio and went to remote parts of the world each summer to dig things up.

His students called him 'Bert'. That is, they called him 'Indiana Bert'. Rather than shy away and be embarrassed by this nickname, he embraced it; 'Indiana Bert' became his alter ego. He bought the costume, including the whip, and wore it for Museum events. This costume only proved to make him more popular, and a whole series of short videos were created explaining the archaeology, or lack of it, behind his hero's movies. So, the hat became a feature of his everyday life as it suited the climate, and although unmarried, Dr Robert Parker-Betts was happy with his life.

On Friday, he had an appointment. The Dog Show was only a week away, and the dog marshalling area would be in the covered, paved area directly outside the Museum. He had received a formal email from Professor Fang, Chair of the Dog Show Planning Committee, requesting the use of this area and assuring him that the Museum would not be entered or damaged.

Then he received a less formal email on a startling email template from Mr Fred Planet of Planet Events, with numerous attachments of plans and schedules and a polite request to meet with Ms Gloriana Groom of Suds-

Mobile. She would be locating a grooming table outside the Museum, and the SudsMobile Salon would be parked close by as per her advertising agreement. Also required was the use of the cleaning cupboard to provide buckets of water in the unlikely event that a 'mishap' should occur.

Indiana Bert had no idea what sort of 'mishap' might occur, but as the caterers would be setting up refreshments in the arcade behind the seating, he assumed someone might accidentally drop a cup of tea. An appointment was made, and Indiana Bert awaited the arrival of Ms Gloriana Groom. He was not yet prepared for the consequences.

Ms Groom was, in fact, a beauty. Her pretty face was irrelevant to her but was essential to enhance her business. She was the heart and soul and very public face of the Suds-Mobile empire-to-be. Her hair was worn loose and straight in an oriental style that showed off her mysterious eyes with their long lashes. She wore a very dark pink Chanel-inspired business suit and alarming pink stilettos. She carried an expensive leather briefcase. She was petite in stature but was quite capable of dominating a room full of basketball players.

Ms Groom focused at all times on her business goals. Precisely on time, she clicked her heels briskly up the steps of the Museum entrance and, smiling her professional smile and firmly shook the hand of the waiting Dr Robert Parker-Betts. There was that wonderful silent moment before the metaphorical Ming vase hit the floor and shattered.

This next paragraph should be italics or some strange rune-like script as a moment when the world stood still. Archaeology and Business collided head-on, and the two froze completely with their greeting smiles still on their lips. Love, at first sight, is, of course, complete rubbish, but sometimes we recognise our soul mate. After that happens, there is not a lot we can do about it.

Suddenly, being six-foot-tall no longer mattered to Indiana Bert, as Ms Groom's wonderful eyes looked incredulously on the face of her hero-to-be. In the background, noisy birds tweeted in the g trees, and the even louder students tweeted on their iPads. But at this moment, our two soul mates-to-be were happily contained in a giant personal bubble of the type seen in adverts for the magical properties of Fairy Liquid.

Then the bubble burst, and the formal business could take place. The plans and schedules were laid out on top of a case of pot shards from ancient Northern Mesopotamia. The two quickly agreed on the grooming table's position, which would be placed over a sizeable empty stone coffin tastefully draped with pink cloth. It was felt that the dogs would not mind too much as it had not been used for some centuries. As it was too large to move, the coffin had remained outside the Museum entrance since it was placed there over a century ago after a bumpy journey from Rome badly chipped the corners.

A key to the cleaning cupboard, discretely hidden behind a Doric column, was entrusted to Ms Groom. Indiana Bert presented his card, and Ms Groom provided him with a bright pink card illustrated with cavorting poodles. He assured her that he would be present that evening, although it clashed with his mother's weekly family dinner, from which he would excuse himself on the grounds of an important event. He was wholly enthusiastic about community use of the University and was happy to be of any assistance. Ms Groom smiled, although she still had no idea why. The man in the hat was not handsome, but he was of a compact and lithe physique and was strangely attractive to her.

The two froze during the final handshake and stared into each other's eyes without quite knowing what was happening. Then Ms Gloriana Groom turned and clicked away.

Their two lives were never going to be the same again.

ELEVEN

Dawn was coming soon. Penny was frozen still. The three Gargoyles remained as stone statues. There had been no movement for two days. Penny was cold and hungry, but she knew if she moved, so would they. She did some calculations and worked out that even if she leapt up and ran for the attic window above, they could probably get to her before she could dive inside.

She looked at the rats' sad remains, once-living creatures, and decided firmly that she would not be the next victim. Of course, she hunted for food, but not like them. She respected her prey and gave each mouse a fighting chance to escape. The Gargoyles were just senseless killers. She thought about Erickson, and Storm and the Eagles, who loved her and imagined their sorrow if she never returned and if they never knew why.

Penny considered that the Gargoyles had the numbers and the speed and the strength; they didn't need to eat or stretch their limbs; they could wait for days, weeks, years even, and she could not. But she had brains and cunning, and she could outsmart them. All she had to do was to wait for a distraction.

If something were to attract their attention, she would have a few precious extra seconds to make it through a window. She very slowly stretched her limbs and flexed her claws. She must be ready to move and fast when the moment came. Clearly, they were not coming for her, or she would already be a pile of lifeless, creamy fur and blood in their claws.

The three Gargoyles had drifted into a state of suspension, somewhere between life and stone. Nothing would hurry them; they had no appointments, and time was firmly on their side. They could, at any moment, wander away and forget Penny, but she was interesting and confusing. Small furry animals ran, sooner or later, in terror and panic, but this one did not. She stayed still and watched them. They had not caught anything like her before. So, they settled down to wait for the next move. They had all the time in the world.

The clock chimed nine o'clock, and it was Monday morning. Indiana Bert was unlocking the Museum side door. The Museum opened to the public at 11 o'clock, and today he would do a complete inspection of the exhibits before the visitors arrived. Sometimes, the conservators were called to inspect an item; sometimes, a fine feather duster was applied to the statues' ornate folds. The display cases were old, and the dark wood shone with years of loving care.

The Museum staff were very proud of their small establishment. The British Museum it was not, but it was looked after with love and enthusiasm. To Indiana Bert, it was the best Museum in the world. He switched on all the lights, collected his notebook and started to inspect the stone sarcophagus. He moved slowly and carefully, and he was in heaven. The things he loved were laid out for his viewing pleasure, and he savoured every minute. Thoughts of the amazing Ms Groom were put aside for a moment.

High above the Museum, Penny suddenly noticed a light come on just a few meters away. She studied carefully and decided that it was probably someone in the rooms below. She reasoned that as it had been very quiet since she arrived, it must have been the weekend, and so now it was Monday, and people were returning to work. She waited and listened. She saw that the light came from a small air vent tucked in the joint between two roof sections, just small enough to let in the fresh air.

If she could get inside, she could hide until it was safe to leave. If she were very lucky, she could drop down into the Museum and escape. But no need to rush, she thought. The Gargoyles still showed no sign of life.

Once all the lights were on, Indiana Bert moved to the Etruscan vases and the cases close to the entrance. From here, he would work his way through ancient Crete and Rome, take a side detour into some odd bits from Cyprus and finally end up in his most-favourite place, Ancient Egypt. He would check each mummy from the smallest mummified cat to the largest High Priest and Pharaoh's second cousin, who was probably his uncle on his mother's side. The temperature was carefully controlled, but the process of mummification was so good that, providing that all was kept dry, things stayed in excellent condition.

Once a year, the mummies went down to the hospital late at night for a full-body scan. This was the only time the scanner was free, and it also avoided terrifying the patients in the waiting area. These were the Museum's most important treasures, and their care was a sacred duty.

In this final room was a small display case of odds and bobs, all mummified for some unknown reason. A baby crocodile, a finger, a foot and a small cat, which had all been preserved for eternity thanks to the mortician's ancient craft. Overhead, two large stone columns supported the Gothic ceiling vaulting, flanked by the stained-glass skylights. Unlike the rest of the Museum that was dark, glossy wood panelling, this area was high, with filtered light and air; it was perfect for displaying the mummies.

Indiana Bert put down his notebook and revolved the display case on the turntable so he could look inside and check the artefacts. And then he made the discovery he had been dreading his whole career. Lying to one side of the linen wrapping was a tiny toe detached from one of the exhibits. There were teeth marks. Something had chewed his mummified cat! Indiana Bert was incoherent for some time.

Penny had been doing her maths and had worked out based on the principle of something to do with speed, distance and the magical ability of a slim cat to slip into a very small gap; she might just make it to the air vent before the Gargoyles could reach her. Still, she waited and watched and listened. The moment would come when the Gargoyles would be distracted for a second or two. She listened to the sounds of someone moving about on the polished wooden floors below her. Looking over at the Gargoyles, they still showed no sign of life; perhaps age had dulled their hearing, or their ears were not carved too well.

Penny was taking no unnecessary chances. She only had nine lives, after all.

Suddenly there was a blood-curdling scream of rage from below, and the Gargoyles sprang to life. This was it! Penny jumped up and dived into the gap, and within a second or two, was falling down inside the air vent, back arched, ready to land gracefully in the room below. By the time Dogface had unfurled his wings and landed at the opening of the duct, Penny was well out of reach. The three Gargoyles settled back into stone and froze on the spot, soaking in their disappointment until their next victim arrived.

Penny landed silently on top of a tall wooden cabinet. She was unnoticed, even though there was an explosion of dust as her paws touched down. On the other side of the room, a man was tearing out his hair and making awful gurgling sounds. Penny thought it best to stay still and hope she was not noticed. He did seem extremely angry, and she needed to locate the way out before she moved again.

Cats do not care about people that much. Either they like them, or they don't like them. It is simple. If a cat likes you, you have either food, warmth, something wriggly on a string, or you give o the right vibrations. Indiana Bert was giving off the right cat-friendly vibrations, but for some reason, he was expressing rage and fury and doing terrible damage to his hair.

Penny watched with surprisingly calm interest. She'd had a fright and spent a couple of cold nights on the roof in danger of being torn to pieces by some ugly winged blocks of stone with nasty attitudes. The top of the cabinet was dusty, but she was safe for the moment and could observe her surroundings while she worked out what was wrong with this funny man. She would take her time and then saunter back to Professor Eagle's office for some food and affection.

Indiana Bert stopped raging and wiped his tears away. He was very, very upset. A precious exhibit had been damaged and it was on his watch too. He gathered up the sad little toe, and the chewed mummy wrappings and placed them carefully in an exhibits box lined with tissue paper. It was time to take them to the conservator and see what she could do to restore the little cat.

He secured the cabinet, all the time thinking about what he should do to prevent more damage. Turning around, he leaned back for a moment and quietly considered who or what might have done this. Rats, mice, termites? The Museum was pretty well protected against that sort of attack. Whatever it was, it had moved the cabinet's turntable and pushed it around to get at the objects. He was silently lost in thought.

The Museum was now opening for the day, and the reception staff were making it ready for the public. The main doors were opened, and a warm gust of air floated inside, so on top of the cabinet, the dust swirled up, and Penny sneezed. Very, very loudly. Indiana Bert looked and saw the animal he thought had caused the desecration of his treasure.

'YOU, YOU,' he was yelling angrily, putting down the precious box and striding to the bottom of the tall cabinet.

Penny looked down at a bright red face and a waving fist, and, being a super-intelligent cat, she had it all worked out in seconds. 'It wasn't me,' she thought, 'but I know who did it'. She decided that it was time to make a speedy exit to consider the situation on top of her comfy book stack.

Indiana Bert was yelling up at her, and before he could think about climbing on a chair and grabbing her, Penny sailed over his head and landed elegantly between him and the main exit.

Then she ran.

TWELVE

That morning, Professor Eagle was conducting a tutorial. Four bright students were sitting in his office discussing the poetry of Algernon Charles Swinburne (1837 to 1909), an alcoholic, once nominated for the Nobel Prize, who pretended to be far more decadent than he actually was. To show that he was very decadent, he wrote about cats and wore startling waistcoats. A student was reading a poem that was then to be discussed by the group.

Stately, kindly, lordly friend, Condescend

Here to sit by me and turn Glorious eyes that smile and burn, Golden eyes, love's lustrous meed, On the golden page I read.

The office door silently drifted open, and Penny sauntered in and casually launched herself onto the book stack on the desk. The student stopped reading and said,

'Hello, Penny.'

Then she remembered that by common consent, Penny was not actually there and should not be mentioned, so she continued with her verses.

Dogs may fawn on all and some as they come;
You, a friend of loftier mind, Answer friends alone in kind. Just your foot upon my hand Softly bids it understand.

Penny stretched, yawned loudly and fell asleep. A gentle smile passed over Professor Eagle's lips, and for the next thirty minutes, they discussed the poem while Penny snored peacefully. Finally, the tutorial ended, and the students trooped out.

'Bye Professor, Bye Penny.'

A delighted Professor reached out his hand to caress the sleek, creamy fur when Penny awoke and sneezed.

And again!

And again!

It was a positively grand sneezing fit. The alarmed Professor raced down the corridor to Storm's office and asked her to come quickly as something was wrong with Penny. Storm hurried down to his room and looked at the frantically sneezing cat just as Professor Poppett's voice boomed along the corridor.

'Call your wife,' said Storm as she spun expertly on her stilettos and raced back to answer the Professorial summons. Professor Eagle, getting more alarmed by the minute, grabbed his phone.

'Is that you, my little Eaglet?' he breathlessly asked the receptionist at the Veterinary School.

'I'll see if she is free,' replied the receptionist, trying not to giggle.

His little Eaglet, who prefer to be called Dr Eagle during surgery hours, came to the phone and, after listening to his frantic message, grabbed her medical bag and a pet carrier, just in case, and made her way swiftly up the hill to her husband's office.

When she arrived, Penny was in a mid-sneezing fit.

Firstly, pulling on some surgical gloves, she gently wrapped Penny in a small towel from her medical bag and wiped her face and eyes. A thermometer was inserted in the usual place, and Penny's eyes bore into her with a sharp look for the indignity. The examination finished; Dr Eagle placed the thermometer in a clean plastic bag and, removing the towel, looked at the layer of dust.

'Where have you been?' she asked Penny while Professor Eagle was sent to fetch some warm water.

Together, the Eagles gently cleaned the ancient dust from Penny's eyes and face. All three seemed to be purring. At last, Penny was pronounced fit and clean and was given a bowl of special food.

'Well, Penny,' said Dr Eagle, 'I don't know where you have been to get into this mess. If you came and lived with us, you would be warm and pampered and totally dust-free.'

Penny eyed the cat box with suspicion. She liked the Eagles, but she was not sure she wanted to go home with them just yet, or ever.

'Up to you, Penny.'

Penny purred contentedly and fell asleep. She was staying right there for the moment.

MEANWHILE, Storm had been issued with a list of unusual tasks.

1. Find a photographer with an excellent reputation to photograph Beloved Poodle performing at the Dog Show.

2. Find earmuffs in the Black Watch Tartan for Poodle to wear for the event.

Storm liked complex tasks, and these were surprisingly easy given some gentle persuasion and a bit of Internet shopping. A quick call to Sweetie of the Pet Couture Department at the House of Dogue told her that ear muffs for dogs were 'much-worn this year by those dogs participating in competitive events'. They were also considered 'essential for the dog travelling by private jet'.

Storm was impressed by Sweetie's sales pitch, but she didn't think Poodle would be jetting off just yet. The Black Watch tartan would tone nicely with Poodle's curly black fur and Professor Poppett's Prada jacket, which was currently sent for dry-cleaning for the big event. Storm placed the order, arranged the courier and hoped Poodle would like the earmuffs.

The next task called for some gentle persuasion and diplomacy. Bruno, the 'photo-artiste', was an international star, but he was also warm and had a terrific sense of fun. Storm was unsure if taking photos at the Dog Show was an assignment that he would even consider. She got on the phone to Erickson, who said, 'Go for it, Darhling' and gave her Bruno's number. When she called, Bruno's recorded message was fast and in Italian. She left a polite message and was not sure she would get a reply.

Twenty minutes later, Bruno called from Cannes, complete with background sounds of clicking paparazzi and a side conversation about a yacht with someone who sounded like George Clooney.

'I will be back home shortly,' said Bruno. 'For you, I will do it. Un sacco di divertimento.'

Storm immediately sent the event's details by email to Bruno and trotted into the Professor with the news. Professor Poppett was amazed and even considered for a split-second giving Storm a pay-rise. A quick glance at Storm's designer stilettos convinced her that it was not necessary. As the door to her office closed, Professor

Poppett thought warmly about Poodle gracing the cover of Celebrity Dog while Storm went to check on Penny.

As she peeped around the door, the Eagles and Penny were folded in a loving tableau.

All was well.

THIRTEEN

The following day dawned bright and clear over the Quadrangle. Everyone was going about the business of fetching their first coffees before a prolonged period of contemplation set in for the day. Professor Poppett arrived at 7am with Poodle bouncing alongside her.

Storm was packing the equipment in a small case on wheels. The list of items: a small stool (Storm, for the sitting on), a clipboard, stopwatch, digital camera, a complete set of regulations and procedures for the obedience section of the Dog Show, dog boots, dog biscuits, bottle of spring water and dog bowl, and a whistle. Storm had no clear indication of what should be worn for a Dog Show rehearsal, so she opted for leather trousers and some startling stiletto-heeled boots paired with a rhinestone trimmed leather jacket. Poodle looked approvingly, and the Professor rolled her eyes as usual at her assistant's eclectic dress sense.

At 7.30am, the three departed for the Quadrangle and set up camp under the arcade. The pristine green of the lawn sprawled temptingly before them. Poodle was kitted out in pink practise earmuffs, formerly worn by the

Professor for her morning run and the dog boots, which were intended to inflict minimum damage to the lawn and keep Poodle's curly toes warm. Storm was inflicting enough damage to the lawn with her heels.

The regulations were studied, and then the Professor and Poodle took their place in the centre of the lawn. Storm blew the whistle and started the stopwatch. With the leash held high, the contestants began a high-stepping routine such as that performed by the Lipizzaner Stallions. It looked very impressive, and many heads were turned to observe. Storm thought that actually only Poodle should be doing the high stepping, but the Professor was so clearly having fun that it seemed a shame to point this out. A few students settled in the sun on the stone walls to watch the show.

From the Gothic entrance to the Quadrangle, two figures appeared nonchalantly walking along the arcade. They wore their hoodies close about their faces and zipped up tight. Oddly, both were wearing grey business suits and incongruous luminous trainers. The words Yo Mutha Fucka embellished on the back of one of the hoodies seemed strangely out of place, given the dark suit peeping out from inside. Their top halves were in the 'hood' and their middles were in the boardroom. On the other hand, their feet were engaged in a basketball game in LA or a hip-hop gig in NY.

The two figures wandered apart and seemed to talk to each other on their mobile phones while separated by a large pillar. No one took much notice of them. It was a university, after all, and no one was supposed to behave normally. Even the Gargoyles didn't bother to wake up, and this time, it would have been a good idea if they had.

Mad Malcolm, for it was he in disguise, clutched a stopwatch close to his chest and was doing a kind of juggling act between it and the clipboard, his pen and mobile phone. The faint shape of an earpiece poked out from under his hoodie. The Dean was hissing instructions down the phone and at the same time was pretending unsuccessfully not to notice Malcolm. Sooner or later, one of them would collide with a large stone column. The conspirators were planning to time the rehearsal of Professor Poppett and Poodle.

In order to do this, they had disguised themselves as students. Well, they thought they had disguised themselves. They did not pay a lot of attention to the current fashions, but a hoodie seemed to be the garment to wear when you wanted to avoid being seen on surveillance cameras. Mad Malcolm had watched a lot of police TV series lately in the hope that Wrinkles might get a part as a sort of female Inspector Rex with shorter legs. He was convinced that the hoodies would make them invisible. It was a bit disap-pointing when students strolled past and said 'Good Morn-ing' to the Dean.

In the centre of the manicured lawn, Professor Poppett and Poodle were delighting the audience with a perfect display of Heel on Leash and Figure Eight, a routine that shows whether the dog has learned to watch and adjust its pace to stay with the handler. Poodle and the Professor looked adoringly at each other as the routine was repeated a few times to allow timings to be noted. Then the second version was rehearsed, Heel and Figure Eight o Leash. The exercise was done a few extra times as Poodle occasionally stopped to admire the Professor's balletic movements in the figure eight. The students applauded enthusiastically in the hope of extra marks for future essays.

This last routine was of special interest to the Dean and Mad Malcolm, as this would be their moment for action, and the timing had to be perfect, or they would be suspected of dirty tricks. Storm scampered forward with a camera to take some quick snaps to send to Bruno to give him a clear idea of his task on the day of the show. Poodle's head tilted towards the camera to ensure a good profile was captured while Storm aerated the lawn with her heels. The Professor was thinking of a special Facebook page to display the photographs. She was sure Storm could find time to do this after lunch.

Finally, Professor Poppett was satisfied with their routine's accuracy, and Storm filled the water bowl with spring water and held out a treat of Saucy Dog Snacks. The Professor did a few laps of the Quadrangle to warm down and a few stretches that impressed the Dean a great deal. Academics were not supposed to be that fit, in his opinion. The Dean and Mad Malcolm then did a strange pacing routine in and out of the Quadrangle.

Malcolm was planning to park his BMW in the space reserved for VIPs, and from the entrance, he calculated he could remain inside the dog marshalling area with his dog and activate his very loud car alarm with the remote unit. The much larger Dean and the Fiend would stand in front of him, so the audience did not see him do it on the day. The students watched with amusement as the two trotted off to the Dean's office for a cup of tea and a muffin, completely forgetting that they were pretending to be students. In the distance, there was a faint shriek from the Dean's Personal Assistant as they entered the office, and another pair of stockings were torn as she leapt up from her desk at the sight of the two hooded men.

ON THE FOLLOWING DAY, several important meetings took place. Early in the morning an email arrived for Storm inviting her to lunch with Bruno and asking if the Professor might be available for an introduction. Storm replied that lunch would be most welcome, and she would arrange for a short interview with the Professor and her Beloved Poodle.

Just before lunchtime, Bruno arrived with a bottle of duty-free Chanel No.5 for Storm. After the happy air-kissing was over, he was ready to meet the Professor. He had a beautifully wrapped gift box with an air of French sophistication oozing from the extravagant bows. Storm knocked at the inner door and announced Bruno was here to say hello. The Professor stood up to greet him, and Poodle sat up, poised to leap in delight.

'Illustre Professore. Piacere di conscerla,' gushed Bruno, seizing the Professor's hand and kissing it.

Poodle bounced forward and pushed a nose into the private part of Bruno's jeans.

'Così Bella,' he said in a high note, suddenly aware of the cold, wet nose and not quite sure what he wanted to say. Professor Poppett was not accustomed to public displays of affection. Still, she did know that to be 'bella' was a good thing, and as Bruno was an international star of the world of fashion, she might make allowances for the hand-kissing, just this once. She reclaimed her hand and did a sort of secret wave to her pet to encourage the removal of the nose. Poodle dropped to a sitting position and considered the box and its lovely ribbon.

Everyone regained their composure, and a little fit of bowing took place as the festooned box was handed over and gratefully received. Bruno had prepared a little speech.

'Signora Professore, I am delighted you have honoured me with an invitation to photograph the triumph of your excellent pet. Be assured Signora Professore, I shall make my best effort.'

Professor Poppett smiled her thanks, being temporarily lost for words. Bruno bowed again. Clearly, someone had told him that bowing was what you did to female professors.

'Ciao, ciao,' he said as the Professor held the gift tightly with both hands so no more kissing could take place. And with another little flourish, Bruno made his exit, leaving a startled Professor to unwrap and eat her gift while Poodle was rewarded with the ribbon to play with. With a quick wink at Storm, he gathered her up for a nice cosy pub lunch and a lovely gossip about his trip to Cannes.

THAT AFTERNOON, Fred Planet had arranged for all the interested parties to view the lawn and seating as the construction began. He had invited Professor Eagle to represent the Judges as Professor Fang, the Chair, was also the President of the Canine Dentistry Association and was attending a tooth cleaning conference.

Mr Thickett, the Head Groundsman, who had been lurking in the area for several days to keep an eye on the lawn, was formally invited to reassure him that no one intended to destroy His Lawn. Dr Eagle attended as the duty veterinarian for the event and Ms Groom as the owner of SudsMobile. All assembled in the lobby outside the Museum as that was to be the dog marshalling area.

Indiana Bert spotted the pink SudsMobile vehicle pull into the VIP parking area directly outside and suddenly found he had to rearrange the display at the Museum entrance. The other staff were quite perplexed when he changed into his leather jacket and brushed his hair before doing this. As he was arranging the souvenir neckties embellished with hieroglyphics, he found it necessary to wander across to the entrance to view the colours in daylight.

Ms Groom, looking splendidly business-like as usual, managed a formal wave of acknowledgement, at which point their eyes locked for somewhat longer than was necessary, causing the rest of the group to follow the direction of her gaze. Indiana Bert then found he was obliged to wave to the rest of the party. An embarrassing moment followed before he retreated behind the reception desk and pretended to do something essential.

After the formal introductions, Fred Planet walked everyone briskly around the area, indicating each section.

'VIP Parking, Dog Marshalling Area, Grooming Station, Veterinary Station, Competitors Entrance, Show Ring, Judges' Podium, Trophy Display, Audience Seating, Exits and Refreshment Area.'

His arms waved with authority, and everyone nodded. The little party then inspected the areas in turn, and Mr Thickett stood gloomily looking down at His Lawn as if it was about to be concreted over. Since that morning, several unexplained small holes had appeared. As his audience were firmly under control, Fred described in complete detail the program of events and handed out printed copies of the running order as it would appear in the souvenir program.

Action 1 - Audience seated

Action 2 - Fanfare (Junior Brass Band)

'In tune, we hope.'

Action 3 - Entrance of the Judges

'Loud applause.'

Action 4 - Introductory Speech by Professor Fang, Chair Action 5 - Vote of thanks to Chair and Introduction of the Trophies by Professor Eagle

Action 6 - Competitors enter from the marshalling area and parade on the lawn with voice-over commentary by Fred Planet

Action 7 - First Competitor >>>> to >>>> Final Competitor

Action 8 - Junior Brass Band interlude: 'A Life on the Ocean Wave' whilst the Judges deliberate

'Inappropriate, but it is their best tune.'

Action 9 - Trophies awarded by Professor Fang

Action 10

Action 10 - Refreshments

Everyone studied the running order carefully while Ms Groom cast a sly glance towards the Museum just as Indiana Bert's head popped up from behind the reception desk. The waving performance was repeated, accompanied by lots of embarrassed smiles. Fred Planet then thanked everyone for their attendance and disappeared to supervise the seating construction.

The Eagles strolled off arm in arm for afternoon tea, and Mr Thickett stood glumly on the lawn as if wishing it farewell.

Ms Gloriana Groom made a sudden decision that a visit to the Museum would be an improving activity. For the first time in her professional life, she trotted off to do something very un-business-like indeed.

FOURTEEN

It was cool and dim inside the Museum but wonderfully calm and tranquil. Indiana Bert was a little shaken by the intense eye contact with Ms Groom and had retreated to the conservator's room to settle himself down. He wanted to check on the restoration of the damaged mummified cat, which he wrongly believed had been horribly mutilated by the intruding feral Siamese. Poor Penny could not defend herself against this accusation just yet, and the idea of mummy-nibbling Gargoyles or any other sort of flesh-eating mythological beasts had not crossed his mind. The sad little cat was cocooned in a box full of tissue while it was drying. The conservator had re-attached the toe and repaired the linen bandages.

Indiana Bert decided he would not return it to the display just yet and had asked for a cotton-wool stuffed sock to be wrapped in linen and made ready to be put on display in place of the authentic object. He would put a label saying, Temporary Replica Exhibit, next to the item until he was sure the mummy would be safe. He was pretty sure that cats could not read, but of course, he had only seen Penny briefly as she sailed over his head and ran for the exit. Her intellectual abilities would make her worthy of a place in any Museum as the most advanced of her species.

The conservator had placed some new items on the workbench, ready for labelling and display. A new project had been recently started when a large box of pottery shards had been discovered in the storeroom. These had arrived in the collection inside other larger objects or at the bottom of the packing cases and were then sorted into trays of various types. The largest box was full of broken pieces of Greek pottery in gorgeous black and reddish colours. These pieces were generally used for study, but on a rainy afternoon, the staff, feeling like doing a jigsaw, had discovered that a lot of the pieces belonged to one large pot.

Conservators employ various non-destructive methods of restoration after analysing the pieces for information about their manufacture and condition. Everyone was very excited. It was decided to fit the pieces together to reassemble the pot using only reversible materials that would not damage the item and could be safely removed later. All had a very satisfying afternoon, and an almost complete pot was assembled, which now sat proudly on the workbench.

Indiana Bert studied it carefully. Despite a few holes, he was confident that it could take its place in the permanent display. It was painted with a slightly naughty frieze of nymphs and gods with well-toned muscles. An almost-whole pot was much more exciting than a box of broken pieces. The glue looked dry, so it might be possible to handle it very soon.

Quivering with excitement, he walked back to the Greek section to look for pots of a similar shape or colouring that might inform his research, and there before his eyes was Ms Gloriana Groom with a curtain of black hair gleaming as it fell across her face. She was studying a display case with some concentration. Indiana Bert felt his heart give a little leap of the sort that usually accompanied an archaeological discovery.

Ms Groom was way out of her comfort zone. This was not business. This was a pleasure. The sort of secret pleasure she had when curled up at home in her pyjamas and slippers amongst her adored Siamese cats. This was a new sensation, and she felt very strange as she saw Indiana Bert's reflection appear in the display cabinet glass, and she saw he was watching her too. She raised her head, and for a moment, the two stared at each other through the glass. To see her image floating among the Greek treasures gave him a slight twinge, and for the first time in her life, Gloriana Groom considered getting herself a man; this man. Someone had to say something and soon.

'Welcome to my Museum,' stammered Indiana Bert and blushed, as it was not technically his Museum. 'Well, not really my Museum, you understand. It's where I, um, live most of the time.'

Indiana Bert was becoming seriously lost for words and in danger of listing himself as an exhibit. Ms Groom looked up, trying to retain a cool appearance even though she was in real danger of tipping off her stilettos. Indiana Bert seized the initiative. He switched quickly to professional curator mode to cover his embarrassment and pointed to the conservator's room's open door.

'Let me show you a new exhibit.'

Gloriana clicked along behind him, a little relieved to be doing something active. They ran out of speed close by the tray containing the sad little cat.

'And there it was,' he growled, explaining the incident

and pointing through the door to the top of the nearest display cabinet.

'It was there.' Indiana Bert was getting his words into a tangle.

'What was there?' asked Ms Groom, looking puzzled.

'A wicked evil exhibit-destroying Siamese cat,' said Indiana Bert furiously.

A very large silent 'O' fell from Ms Groom and clattered on the polished wooden floor.

Indiana Bert felt he might have dug a trench and fallen in to it quite accidentally. Ms Groom's very pretty eyes looked hurt, and he was afraid he had damaged something priceless. She twirled a little on her heels and, not wishing to distress him further, whispered, 'I have four Siamese myself, but I do assure you, Dr Parker-Betts, it was not one of mine.'

Indiana Bert grasped the opportunity to climb out of the trench.

'Really, four Siamese? My mother has the fluffy type, you know. I prefer Siamese, of course. Like yours, of course, as they won't be ill-disciplined cats that eat my exhibits.'

Sensing they were now on safe ground, Indiana Bert moved to the bench to show her the new pot. Forgetting he had not been told that it could be examined and wanting to show his professional skills, he pulled on a pair of white cloth gloves left on the bench and gently lifted the pot for her to admire. He had a very uncomfortable feeling that he had made a terrible mistake. The pot was almost but not yet completely dry. It was now stuck to the gloves. On the other side of the workshop, a couple of conservators watched the little scene to see how Indiana Bert would get himself out of this situation. The glue was designed to be removed, and the pot could be reassembled, so there was no need for a big fuss.

Indiana Bert frantically searched for his next move.

Like the true professional he was, he started to describe to her the scene depicted on the pot before he had carefully observed what it was.

'Red-figure vases were exported throughout Greece and beyond,' he began. He looked down and saw the detail on the pot, now firmly stuck to his fingers and turned a difficult shade of red.

'Er as you can see, this is the God, Hermes, wearing a, a, a, nothing but a very short cloak and some sandals.' He is, um er um chasing the nymph, um, in order to um um. Oh My!'

Gloriana tried to look seriously interested despite her quivering mouth. The conservators exchanged glances and decided the Indiana Bert was a lovely guy, and he should be rescued from his embarrassing situation. One of them strode across the workshop and expertly inserted his hand inside the pot and gently pulled it out of Indiana Bert's grasp, taking the gloves with it. He then replaced the pot right way up on the workbench, with the white gloves still glued fast at either side, like forlorn rabbit ears.

'Thank you,' said Indiana Bert briskly to fill the silence.

Ms Groom felt it was now up to her to restore his dignity. She reached out a delicately manicured hand and took hold of his now gloveless fingers.

'No. Thank you for a fascinating talk,' she said in her best brisk, business voice as she shook his trembling hand.

Then she turned expertly on her heels and clicked away, tossing her hair aside and looking over her shoulder. Then she smiled.

'Thank you so much.'
Then she disappeared through the door to the exit.

FIFTEEN

Dr Robert Parker-Betts had a lot to mull over, as he stood motionless for an hour holding the injured pot while the conservator removed the gloves and cleaned up the sticky residue. He then treated everyone to a pizza dinner to make up for his terrible misdemeanour.

The restored pot, not that it was ever in real danger, sat plumply in the workshop with a large sign reading, Do Not Handle, displayed in front of it so there would be no more mistakes. The Museum staff were quietly delighted at the little love affair blooming in front of them.

Indiana Bert had devised a plan to capture the defiler of his precious mummy and had chosen the evening when the alluring Ms Groom would be around to be casually asked out for dinner following the Dog Show. The dummy mummy, which consisted of an old sock wrapped in some old pieces of linen from the storeroom, would be put back in the display cabinet. Some small pieces of fish would be tucked inside to give a tempting odour.

Indiana Bert would then leave the Museum front door slightly open during the Dog Show and hide somewhere inside close to the display case and wait for the wicked feral Siamese to try for another nibble of the little cat mummy. He would have a cage ready for capture, and once he had caught this menace, it would be handed over to the vet school for disposal. By disposal, he meant a nice home somewhere far away. This plan would provide him with an important reason to be around that particular evening and, hopefully, a good tale to tell at their intimate dinner.

The next evening, he decided he needed some advice, and as his father was somewhere in the wilds of Canada, he had dinner with his mother. Dinner in the Parker-Betts household was a formal repast with cats. His mother decanted herself from the sofa and, dressed in a cat-fur embellished black dress from the 6os, made a sort of royal progression to the dining room with her son trailing behind carrying the tray of takeaway Thai food.

A bottle of wine was excavated from under the gardening tools in the cellar. Indiana Bert put the tray down, formally arranged his mother in her chair, then pulled the cork and tasted the vintage.

There was a sort of 'whoosh' as the pile of cats on the sofa realised that their mistress had relocated to another place in which food was being served, and the entire heap of fur dived under the dining table and draped themselves around her feet. Exactly how many cats was never quite clear as the fur extended far beyond their actual bodies. Indiana Bert had the uncomfortable feeling that his formal trousers would be paying another expensive trip to the dry cleaners to get de-furred.

His mother dished out the dinner with the silver utensils from her family cutlery box, and then both settled down to a comfortable meal. They were content in each other's company, and the only distraction was the occasional claw in the leg as the below-table diners pressed their claim to another prawn. An extra portion of food was purchased for this, so there was plenty for all. A chorus of deep purrs rose to meet the gentle notes of an opera playing in the background on the radio. There was a short yowling contest between cats and sopranos, but no one took much notice.

After the green tea ice cream was eaten and the foil containers were placed under the table to be licked clean, Indiana Bert thought it was time to seek his mother's advice.

'Mother,' he said gently, 'how would you feel if I married? That is, if I asked someone to marry me and if she said yes and so on.'

His mother looked appalled.

'Oh Bobsy, that is a dreadful thing to do. You are so young.'

He was thirty-five. He gently reminded his mother of his advancing years, his excellent job and settled lifestyle. A wife would be a glorious addition to his life.

'I remember your first discovery,' his mother mused. 'Your father was so puzzled by your choice of career and kept banging on about scientific advancement. Silly man. I thought it was ever so clever of you to dig up all those old people in Cairo.'

His mother was clearly not quite ready for this step, so Indiana Bert tried another approach.

'I expect you would like some grandchildren, Mother.'

His mother looked as if he had announced he was buying a couple of Rottweilers that would romp around the gardens terrifying her cats.

'My babies would not be keen on that idea, my dear. I suppose we could buy the house across the road and you could all live there. She would like cats, of course. I could leave her my pearls. Would she come to dinner very often, do you think?'

His mother, as always, got the essential issues sorted out first. When she was confident that Bobsy's wife would be a cat-lover and frequent dinner guest and would be happy to live across the road, she inquired if he had anyone in mind or if he was going to start a search for a suitable wife. She seemed to regard the process as requiring a trip to Egypt in the hope of excavating someone appropriate.

Indiana Bert was very fond of his mother, and her irresponsible parenting style had allowed for a happy, free and stimulating childhood. She was often lost in the library for hours on end.

'I have someone in mind, Mother,' he confessed.

'Well, I supposed you had better marry her, dear, if you like her. She will be very welcome.'

'Thank you, Mother.'

His mother, as usual, left him to make up his mind, having dispensed her unconditional love and total lack of curiosity about his bride to be.

Indiana Bert had made the first step towards matrimony.

SIXTEEN

Penny had not left the safety of Professor Eagle's office since her horrible encounter with the Gargoyles. The Professor's office looked out onto an internal courtyard, and he left a small window open so she could slip down the drainpipe and wander in the tropical garden below. She had an interesting encounter with a tiny succulent mouse, but after enjoying a short chase, she merely batted it around gently then let it go. Her taste for live food had completely disappeared for now. The memory of the hideous Gargoyles ripping the poor rats apart was stuck in her mind, and she was considering becoming a feline pescatarian if she could find a nice pond nearby. She had heard that ornamental carp were fun to catch and highly nutritious.

As she dozed on the window ledge, impervious to the drop below, she considered how she might put right the awful accusation made by the crazy man in the Museum. If word got out that she was responsible for such a desecration, her happy free life on campus might be at risk. Right now, everyone accepted her presence, but that could change if she were thought to be eating the Museum exhibits. She had to work out a plan after the next catnap or two. Penny closed her eyes and purred herself to sleep.

Across town, a posh dinner party was in progress. Mad Malcolm was comfortably seated at the elegant dining table of Mrs Dean, the blonde former actress who had been selected by the Dean to supervisor his domestic arrangements while she 'rested' from her slightly sparkly stage career. She showed off the embroidered muzzle, which was to be worn by the Fiend as a condition of his participation in the Dog Show. The Dean looked proudly at his beautiful and elegant wife as he admired her needlework. If she weren't such a bore, his life would be perfect.

As dessert was finished and coffee announced in the drawing-room, there was a very real danger that Mrs Dean would be accompanying herself on the pianoforte for the delight of her guests, as she reprised her starring role in a Sondheim classic. She conveniently forgot to mention that she was actually the understudy for this particular production. She had rehearsed all the songs, and now she was 'darn well gonna sing'. Her remote Southern accent was present in her thoughts, if not in her public, implied Canadian persona.

'I am so sorry to leave you all,' said the Dean to his guests,' pressing University business must take precedence over your delightful company.'

And with a nod towards the Director of University Buildings and a formal bow to his wife, who glared back with a smile through her cosmetically whitened teeth, he and Mad Malcolm withdrew to the library.

The running order for the Dog Show was laid out on the table with plans for the seating. Mad Malcolm had noted the timings for each item and had discovered that

Professor Poppett and Poodle would be the final contestants to perform their obedience exercises.

The Heel on Leash and Figure Eight exercise took two minutes, and then there was another minute before they would commence the Heel off Leash and Figure Eight. That was the moment when they would act. Poodle would be off the leash and seated as the Professor positioned herself to begin the Figure Eight movements with Poodle unrestrained by her side. They expected to have a clear line of sight from the marshalling area, but just in case, it would be precisely at the moment when they announced 'Begin' for the final exercise. Poodle would be close to the trophy table placed to one side of the Judge's Podium. If startled, there was a good chance that an alarmed leap from an animal as big and bouncy as Poodle would knock over the trophies, and mayhem would follow. The beast would be disqualified!

Mad Malcolm had a special remote to set off his car alarm. Once Poodle had run amuck, the alarm had pre-set timings or could be silenced remotely. The two conspirators would not be expected of foul play, and one of them was sure to win the competition, if not on merit, then by default. They rehearsed the actions a couple of times and then retired for a game of billiards. The sound of Mrs Dean launching into *Send in the Clowns* wafted along the corridor.

Meanwhile, back on campus, a less elegant meal was taking place in the Union Bar. Fred Planet had spent the day watching Mr Thickett wring his hands in agony as small pieces of lawn were expertly removed by one of his staff to allow for the support legs of the audience seating to be erected on the lawn. This was done with surgical precision, and the extracted portions placed on large seed trays to be kept in controlled conditions for later replanting. For Mr Thickett, Head Groundsman and custodian of all things green, it was like having his toenails removed. He watched intently less the procedure injured one blade of grass.

Fred could not bear it any longer and invited Mr Thickett to partake of a pint of something delicious and a Pie Floater in a quiet corner of the bar. This iconic dish, consisting of a round meat pie served upside down in a bowl of thick pea soup topped with tomato sauce, Worcestershire sauce or vinegar, is traditionally eaten standing up by the pie cart.

There was no actual cart, as the students were not keen on standing up. It reminded them that one day they too would have to go to work, so the pair ate seated at a bar table.

Fred had not realised that Mr Thickett was the author of the *History of Lawns in New South Wales*, which had sold ten copies on eBay in a recent public attack of lawn enthusiasm. Shortly after the first pint, Fred realised that he was to be the lucky recipient of Mr Thickett's lecture on lawn care, which was once delivered to a gardening program on the radio. It came deliciously laced with Latin names pronounced carefully in Mr Thickett's broad accent. It did seem to calm Mr Thickett considerably, especially as he sensed that Fred was unlikely to remember an important appointment and was, therefore, free to enjoy the whole lecture and not just the sound bite version.

Sometime later, Fred realised that his companion had stopped speaking and was looking at him and waiting for some applause.

'Brilliant,' said Fred Planet, feeling fully awake for the first time in an hour. He hoped he was not required to ask questions as he had gone off lawns for the foreseeable future.

'Another pint, Mr Thickett?' he asked, hoping to create a diversion.

The empty pint glass was handed over. Mr Thickett observed his captive.

'Another one of those floaters would be agreeable,' he said.

SEVENTEEN

That night, much higher up and in a far darker place, the three Gargoyles were drifting steadily out of their state of suspension. Stone limbs and organs were drawing nourishment from their organic origins and slowly drifting back to life. Eyes that had seen things too terrible to speak of out loud were raising their heavy stone eyelids. The Gargoyles had unfinished business, and they were waking up and flexing their claws. Dogface unfurled his wings and sniffed horribly. They were not in a good mood, but then they seldom were. The strange creature had escaped from them, and their pride was dented somewhat.

Dragonclaw, with his long tail and huge claws, writhed very slowly as his stone entrails came to life and pained him. Fishbeak shook his great head as if the annoyance of having a fish carved in his beak for eternity was more than he could stand, and he was preparing to explode with frustration. It was up to him to organise the next assault on the Museum, and the others were going to need encouragement. They could easily sink back into stone and stay there for a couple of hundred years. He slowly slithered to the edge of the stone parapet where he sensed movement, and ignoring the squawking and shrieking of the adult birds circling around, he removed in his talons an entire nest of small wriggling fledglings and placed in the centre of the assembled Gargoyles.

'Yuck dems babies,' complained Dragonclaw, breathing a foul stench over the terrified birds. Overhead, the adult birds were working up to a frenzy while not daring to get too close even to rescue their offspring.

Dragonclaw reached out a long claw to extract one of the small snacks. The tiny birds screamed in fear and clung together in the centre of the nest. He lifted a tiny, frightened bird up and away from its siblings and regarded the trembling body with amusement. Sensing a terrible fate awaited them all, the other fledglings, instead of waiting to be dismembered, decided to test their new flight feathers. It was now, or all that evolution would go to waste.

The birds flapped their wings madly and, with one rush, got airborne and headed straight up towards the claw holding their little fellow. Dragonclaw instinctively opened his claw to grab them all and let go of his grip on the first bird, who realising he was falling, started to beat his wings, got airborne and threw himself o the roof in what would be his first, or possibly, his last flight. The others followed and swooped to the ground, landing in a heap in the middle of the lawn. The adult birds landed close by to protect them and ushered the whole family to the safety of the nearest large patch of shrubbery. High above, Dragonclaw shredded the nest in a fury. The meeting had not made a very good beginning.

Fishbeak decided to call the meeting to order, and after tapping his huge claws to command attention, he nodded to

Dogface to report on the last meeting and the plan of action.

He, of course, could not talk due to the inconvenient fish in his beak and was reduced to a series of horrible squawks and grunts. There were a lot of unattractive noises that were presumed to be a sign of order.

'At the last meeting, it was decided that a further investigation of the deceased creature will be carried out on the evening of the Dog Show. The Museum is likely to be unoccupied, and everyone will be watching the show. I propose that we use this opportunity to remove the item from the display for the purposes of, um, er, scientific research.'

There was a lot of claw tapping at this point, which usually meant, 'yes' or 'I am fed up and will rip out your liver presently'. Dragonclaw, still very cross about the loss of the avian snacks, addressed the meeting in his irritating fashion.

'I fink that wes getted sums snaks that nights hehehe. Maybees they dont keeps dems eyes on the little doggies as dems is busy watchin the big uns. Hehehe. Doggies is wery nice, tanks yus.'

The others gave him a knowing look as they recalled the fuss over the last little dog that went missing. A former Professor of Mathematics had furnished himself with a young wife. The lovely Jane was the daughter of a naval officer from Plymouth. She arrived with a vocabulary of seafaring epithets, a quantity of whalebone corsetry and flouncy petticoats.

After his marriage, the Professor spent a lot more time in his office doing research. It was the lady's custom, after a small drop of gin at lunch, to fall asleep in an armchair on the lawn with her Pekingese warmly settled in her lap. It was from this ample lap that Dragonclaw, one hundred years earlier, had plucked the small dog. Jane awoke just in time to see her beloved pet vanish in the claws of a monster, and she fainted clean away.

When revived by some passing academics, her story was not believed, and she was accused of being drunk. Fearing his wife would be sent to an asylum and his reputation destroyed, the Professor sent her to Tasmania to recover.

Following his sudden death, a year later, his estate was valued at a staggering eight thousand pounds and was left to his three sons. He left an annuity of £80 to his estranged wife, provided that she did not return to the University. The keeping of Pekingese was not encouraged after that.

Dragonclaw looked at the others with his drooling fangs, and it was not too hard to work out what he was thinking. The Pekingese had been the high point of his century.

The meeting was called to vote by a prolonged growl from Fishbeak, who was in the chair.

'All those in favour say, 'Aye,' said Dogface.

He glared round in case of disagreement, and each tapped a claw in assent. Then, the night being very dark and silent, the three Gargoyles thrashed their wings, and each flew off to a different rooftop to rest.

EIGHTEEN

The morning of the Dog Show dawned bright and clear. The sun peeked out from behind the clock tower at 5.25am. The warm climate allowed for early evening events in the summer, and a 5pm start was planned. By the interval time, the hungry audience would eat anything the caterers chose to offer them, and it was too early for anyone to get seriously drunk unless they brought their own ask.

There was also another more delicate reason regarding the prevention of 'mishaps.' The dogs had been fed that morning, so for the duration of the show, they would be well behaved and delighted by the little encouraging treats offered by their handlers. A few puddles were the most likely 'mishaps', and it was thought the lawn would benefit. An anxious Mr Thickett was up early, inspecting his lawn and snipping off renegade strands of grass from the pristine carpet.

Fred Planet was awake and typing out his commentary on his iPad as he conjured up witty puns and sayings to amuse the audience. He hoped a career in radio might beckon once his mellifluous tones were heard in public.

Bruno started his day with a run along the beach with his trainer. His happy, active life demanded peak fitness to complement his celebrity status. The evening's assignment was well below his usual type of event, but he hoped it might add some attractive, quirky shots to his portfolio. He might even branch out into celebrity pet portraits. The Professor's funny Poodle would provide some amusing photos. He would have a late lunch and a nice nap before dressing in his customary black jeans, T-shirt and designer trainers before making his way to the University.

The Dean was nursing a hangover while his wife performed her morning vocal exercises alfresco. No matter how many fat pillows he pulled over his head, he could not blot out the sound of her strident trilling coming from the patio. This wife had been a poor choice, he thought to himself. The Fiend was ripping up the flowerbeds as no one had given him his breakfast.

Mad Malcolm started late that morning due to his overindulgence the night before. Too much chocolate pudding made him slow and grumpy. Wrinkles was ready for her walk and had fetched her lead and was pushing it under the duvet to get her owner to wake up. There was nothing like a cold, wet leather dog lead, not to mention the scratchy buckles and chain to get her master's full attention. Mad Malcolm groaned and got up.

Storm slept peacefully, anticipating a busy day ahead. Attending a Dog Show was not in her job description, but it might be fun. She would wear her striking leather pants and matching jacket and some sensible boots, as getting stuck in the lawn again would be just too embarrassing. A trip to Erickson's shop might be called for, and she gave some thought to a new handbag.

In Professor Poppett's apartment, the alarm had gone

off at precisely 4.30am as the Professor was going to row up the harbour with her rowing team before returning to wake Beloved Poodle for a brisk walk around the park and a healthy organic dog breakfast. Ms Groom would visit later to give Poodle a herbal shampoo, clip and toenails before the dog's early afternoon nap. Professor Poppett had prepared a schedule of the day's activities that Storm had typed and uploaded to her iPad and made copies for everyone, including the fridge door.

The Eagles breakfasted on the balcony of the Eyrie. They wore 'His and Hers' matching tracksuits and looked lovingly at one another during the muesli. Professor Eagle had prepared his speech, which was a slightly adapted version of his welcome speech at the last Long Eighteenth Century conference. Dr Eagle had packed her medical kit and prepared her newest navy-blue veterinary uniform, which her husband found quite alluring. Their day would be spent enjoying each other's company.

Ms Groom was up early for her daily swim. She had a long list of clients to see before driving to the University to set up her grooming station on top of the stone con. She was looking forward to the event and had an ample supply of pretty pink advertising material ready for display. She was expecting to gain some new clients after the evening's show and particularly wished for one of her clients to be the winner. The photograph could then be added to her website. Briefly, her thoughts drifted to Dr Parker-Betts, and she imagined spending the digging season in an exotic location once she had SudsMobile successfully franchised. He was handsome, and although a little older than her original specifications for a mate, his impressive scholarly achievements would be advantageous. She thought she was unlikely to be bored in his company.

Meanwhile, Indiana Bert was up at his usual time and enjoying a jolly breakfast with his mother, who seemed to think he was attending a show of mummified dogs and was concerned it would be sad for him. He explained the Dog Show in detail, but she still seemed to think the dogs were archaeological. Smiling at his delightful and sometimes peculiar parent, he went to spend a couple of happy hours cleaning his motorbike.

Later, he would bathe and dress in his leather jacket and Indiana hat ready for the evening. He rather hoped that Ms Groom would find him very manly and attractive, and he could take her out to an informal dinner. He had an idea that she might be a bit doggy after her evening's work and would prefer a pie at Harry's Cafe de Wheels rather than dinner at the posh Japanese restaurant. He would have his dinner suit cleaned for their first formal date. He polished the chrome mudguards frantically in an attempt to distract himself from any further thoughts of the developing relationship and what might be revealed when Ms Groom discarded her tight, pink SudsMobile uniform.

The Gargoyles did not attempt to move. They were indifferent to the time of day or the weather. The glorious morning sunshine was of no interest to them.

Penny rolled over on the Professor's comfy chair, purred and went back to sleep.

NINETEEN

It was time to begin. Everyone was arriving and wandering around the cool arcades of the University Quadrangle. Ms Groom was doing some last-minute brushing and fluffing, and all the owners were giving their dogs their important final instructions. She was beautifully dressed in her pink uniform with the practical addition of pink wellies and a frilly apron.

Soon everyone would take their seats; the Junior Brass Band would play the fanfare, and the Judges, wearing formal attire or, in Professor Eagle's case, his academic gown, would process and mount the podium. The Chair would make his speech of welcome, with jokes craftily harvested from online joke sites, and then Professor Eagle would give his thanks to the Chair, explain the various trophies and thank their sponsors and donors. An air of anticipation settled over the Quadrangle.

The trophies stood on the neatly draped table for all to see in the front of the podium. There were many small prizes, such as Best-Behaved Dog, Best Juvenile, but the two big awards were Best in Show, and Best-Groomed Dog and

Handler. Both these awards boasted colossal silver cups, and everyone wanted to win, not one but both, as this had never been done before. A cute little pink ribbon sat at a jaunty angle on the handle of the Best-Groomed trophy. If you looked closely, the label read, Proudly Sponsored by SudsMobile. Ms Groom understood the power of promotion.

In the marshalling area, the contestants were reporting to the stewards, and Dr Eagle was taking a final look to make sure the dogs were all healthy and fit to perform. The Dean was wearing a type of American basketball jacket embroidered by his wife with the Faculty crest. This design also decorated the Fiend's muzzle. They walked up and down on the flagstones, growling quietly to themselves.

Mad Malcolm and Wrinkles had arrived in Wrinkle's smart BMW, that was now parked close by in the VIP area. Mad Malcolm took this to be an event that needed an aristocratic touch, and he was attired in a sort of huntin' shootin' & fishin' jacket as worn by members of the Royal Family. The very large pockets would hide the bulky remote for the car alarm. Wrinkles was sitting on a low stone wall on her Burberry rug that protected her wrinkly bottom from the cold. Mad Malcolm hoped he would be mistaken for someone very important, and Wrinkles, in dog thoughts, was thinking the same.

Various other contestants were brushing their dogs, and all were chatting happily. There was a splendid Dutch Barge Dog that kept blocking the exit and was picked up and placed in another position by its devoted owner as if it was a piece of furniture. The dog was quickly losing the will to walk as it was picked up so often, this being easier than manoeuvring it into the correct place. Two fabulous fluffy apricot poodles were posing for selfies with their giggling owners. Finally, Professor Poppett and Poodle arrived, and everyone cast an envious eye over their splendid outfits. The Professor was wearing jodhpurs and riding boots with a Prada jacket in Black Watch tartan.

GASPS!

They certainly would make the pages of Horse and Hound if a photograph were submitted. Poodle's fur curled and shone, and the beautifully brushed ears were crowned with earmuffs in a matching tartan. Poodle did tend to leap if surprised, and as the Professor directed her dog by a series of elegant hand signals, there was no need for Poodle to hear at all. Also, nice warm ears made for a happy dog. Storm trotted behind them, having settled for black and white wellington boots adorned with little Scotties to complement her leather outfit. Team Poodle was certainly putting on a show.

Bruno came over and bowed formally to the Professor. He was bedecked with cameras and was already enjoying himself by taking candid shots of the contestants. The caterers were feeding him complimentary cupcakes. The Professor and Poodle were indeed Celebrity Dog material. He winked at Storm, who sensed another nice lunch might be coming up soon.

Then Fred Planet moved to the microphone and announced that it was time for everyone to take their seats. He sprayed his throat to ensure his tones were the required honeyed consistency. Once all were seated, He introduced the Junior Brass Band and the entrance of the Judges.

Someone in the University hierarchy once had the bright idea that the university staff's children were particularly talented at the playing of brass instruments. A band was formed, and uniforms, displaying the crest of a lion rampant mounting a jacaranda tree, were purchased.

Unfortunately, all these careful preparations, and the employment of a part-time bandmaster, could not persuade the children to play in tune, or together. Their adoring parents were very keen that all formal events should include a fanfare and musical interlude by their little prodigies. Those in the know had earplugs ready as twelve children of various sizes and ages stomped onto the lawn in a vaguely marching formation and began to play a ceremonial flourish.

'AND NOW, LADIES AND GENTLEMEN, PLEASE PUT YOUR HANDS TOGETHER FOR THE JUDGES OF TONIGHT'S COMPETITION.'

Professor Fang led the procession, wearing his official jacket adorned with little doggy incisors. Professor Eagle followed him, his hair neatly brushed and wearing his black academic gown. Lastly, filling the gender equality position, Ms Von Katten, the community representative, was handed up the steps by a marshal, and the three took their seats on the Judges' podium. Before them, the lawn shimmied like a green velvet dress, and they had a direct view of the contestants and the audience seated opposite.

The official speeches and polite applause were quickly over, and the dogs were ready to commence the grand parade. The Junior Brass Band thumped off and headed for the sticky fattening trays of refreshments it was thought appropriate to give to them to stop them wandering off before the next musical interlude.

All were in place, and it was time to begin, so Professor Fang started by explaining the rules.

'The handler will enter the ring with the dog on a loose leash and stand with the dog sitting in the heel position. I will ask if the handler is ready before giving the order to begin. The handler may give a command or signal to heel and will walk briskly and naturally with the dog on a loose leash. The dog must not interfere with the handler's freedom of motion at any time. At each order to halt, the handler will stop. The dog shall sit straight and promptly in the heel position without command or signal and shall not move until the handler again moves forward on my order.'

Bruno padded gently to the front of the audience seating. He framed his shots like a true professional, quietly, methodically and always with an eye on the elusive award-winning photograph and a big pay cheque. There was polite applause for each contestant, especially the Dutch Barge Dog, who sat down twice and had to be picked up. The apricot poodles flirted with the Judges like naughty schoolgirls.

Last to appear was Professor Poppet and Poodle, and in true drum majorette marching style, they paraded with heads held high, and in Poodle's case, ears flapping in the breeze. The audience applauded and murmured their approval.

'She ain't half posh,' said one admirer. .

The Dean and Mad Malcolm, having completed their circuits, observed Team Poodle in annoyance and secretly smirked. A figure resembling a member of some tragic Greek chorus was hovering to one side of the audience and wincing in pain each time a heavy foot was placed on the lawn. It was going to be a very long evening for Mr Thickett. Then the parade concluded, and the competition began.

'AND THE FIRST CONTESTANT IS...' announced Fred Planet, trying to sound like a combination of a famous cricket commentator and Billy Crystal.

Each competitor was required to complete a Heel on Leash and Figure Eight. This exercise was performed while the dog was still on the leash, and marks were awarded for obedience and style as well as for the condition and grooming of the dog and handler.

The real test came with the second exercise, the Heel off Leash and Figure Eight. The handler walked to the other side of the show ring while the dog remained seated until commanded to come to heel at his handler's command. Then the two performed a walking figure of eight in perfect synchronisation. The marks here were much higher as the dog was untethered, and lots of extra marks were given for interpretation and poise. Some dogs in this situation simply wandered off and piddled in the corner.

The Fiend and the Dean performed rather well, despite the whistles from his wife, who thought she was back at the Dallas Cowboys. For Wrinkles, this was just another trophy or two she was bound to win, and the air of nonchalance did look a little like boredom. The Dutch Barge Dog got to the seated position and fell asleep. His long-suffering owner, who now had a backache, was glad when it was over and carried him off.

Finally, Professor Poppett and Poodle were ready to perform. The Professor posed in the entrance to Bruno's absolute delight as he framed the shot. Everyone looked admiringly at her command and poise. It was rather like one of the Valkyries had come alive and, discarding her helmet with the horns, was about to launch into her big aria. There was a hush as the two moved forward in perfect formation and coordinating Black Watch tartan.

They completed the Heel on Leash and Figure Eight to a tremor of applause. After waiting for the Judge's command to continue, Poodle was positioned at one end of the lawn while the Professor moved into her starting position on the other side.

This was the moment of truth. Would Poodle stay and wait for the call to heel? There was a silent moment of anticipation as everyone held their breath. The Professor gave her hand signal, and Poodle stood, came to attention and began to walk steadily towards her. It was perfect; it was elegant, and all eyes were firmly on the two contestants as Poodle turned to assume the heel position behind the Professor.

Suddenly the shriek of a car alarm ripped apart the silence!

TWENTY

You must now wait, dear Reader, because we have to go back a couple of hours. Things are happening inside the Museum, and Penny is awake and on the move. Professor Eagle was getting ready for the Dog Show, so it was easy for Penny to slide down the drainpipe unobserved and out into the courtyard. She was not planning on a trip to the rooftops anytime soon after her nasty fright. There were a lot of students wandering about, so it was easy to slip in amongst them and walk unnoticed to the Museum.

As she turned into the Quadrangle, she saw a pretty woman in bright pink wellingtons arranging a series of brushes and combs on top of a con draped with a pink-plastic sheet. Neatly displayed were brochures and signs advertising SudsMobile. A cat like Penny can read, of course. She concluded that the woman washed dogs, which was a most necessary service, in Penny's opinion. Only cats were sufficiently intelligent to clean themselves decently.

Out on the lawn, she could see an elderly man sitting forlornly stroking the grass like it was a pet, and another man was fussing around, giving orders to a collection of younger men and women in long black aprons. Tables were being prepared, and trophies polished. Away in the distance, she saw the familiar figure of Dr Eagle with her medical bag coming towards her. Remembering the thermometer, Penny slid around the open door and into the Museum. She sunk into the gloomy interior and checked carefully around her.

A few late visitors were taking selfies with the bottoms of the Greek statues. Penny padded quietly to the Egyptian display. There was an alcove into which a tall cabinet was neatly fitted. The cabinet was the sturdy wooden type with a broad lower section containing the exhibits. These were accessed by way of a revolving turntable. Between the top of the cabinet and the apex of the alcove, there was a small gap.

Penny leapt expertly to the top of the cabinet and tucked herself into the gap. Thankfully, it had been dusted quite recently. From here, she could look down on the display. She could see the little mummified cat and the new label placed in front of it saying Temporary Replica Exhibit. Penny had a little think. The man who was so very upset must have replaced the original mummified cat with a replica to keep the real one safe. The Egyptian cat was safe, and this was a duplicate. Actually, it was an old sock stuffed with cotton wool and wrapped in yellowing bandages.

It was late afternoon, and the golden sun poured in through the stained-glass windows, turning the shafts of light to blue and green. Penny made sure she was out of sight and hopefully out of reach if a giant claw tried to grab her, and then she settled down for a catnap. There were plenty of humans around, so she felt reasonably safe for the moment.

After a time, when the last of the visitors had left, there

was the sound of sturdy shoes, and the bad-tempered man came in wearing a leather jacket and a hat. He looked rather exciting, like a film star. He was carrying a tin of sardines and a small cage. Penny watched as he spun the display case around and took out the replica cat. He then placed the cage between the wooden legs of the cabinet and pushed it out of sight. He prised open the linen bandages and spooned some sardines from a tin inside the bundle.

'Bait,' thought Penny in disgust, 'I am supposed to eat those sardines.'

This was not likely, as Penny's palate had evolved far beyond most felines. Braised tuna with Hollandaise and green beans, but sardines from a tin? I don't think so. Indiana Bert removed the temporary sign and closed the cabinet. Then he went across to the wooden painted Mummy case standing nearby. It was lavishly painted with gold decorations of Egyptian funeral scenes showing the jackal-headed god Anubis. It stood upright to show off the paintings and was about six feet high. Indiana Bert opened the front, and Penny could see the case was empty.

He examined the section around the painted face and blew the dust out of two holes drilled through the painted eyes. The previous owner had drilled two holes to spy on his manservant from inside the case. When he finally jumped out, he was so excited that he had a heart attack, and his manservant had an excellent story to tell in the servant's hall. Indiana Bert checked the hinges and rubbed a little oil over them.

'Ah, he is going to hide in there,' thought Penny.

There was a sound of more people arriving outside the Museum, and Penny could smell the nasty musty odour of dogs. Indiana Bert kept wandering to the main door and peeping around it as if he was watching someone. Penny suspected the lady in pink was the subject of his observations. Finally, he closed the Museum door, so just a crack was open and then turned o all the lights. To the casual observer, the Museum was closed. It said so on the door.

Then he returned to the Mummy case, got inside and slowly closed the door. 'Now we wait,' thought Penny. Outside, the sound of people and dogs was getting more intense. There was laughter and the clicking of cameras and the occasional toot of a trumpet. Then there was the awful sound of a lot of brass instruments playing out of tune. Penny believed it was called a fanfare but had no idea why. Then, all was quiet, and the sound of amplified voices murmured in the background for a long time, punctuated by the occasional burst of polite applause.

Penny knew that the bad-tempered man thought she was the one who had damaged the exhibits, and now she must find a way to show him he was wrong.

Meanwhile, on the roof, three very grumpy Gargoyles had roused themselves and were heading for the stone pillars that descended into the Museum. There had been a very serious quarrel about who was in charge, and giant wings were raised in an attempt to intimidate. As Dragonclaw was the biggest, Fishbeak and Dogface both agreed that it was best to let him go first, as he would be unbearable for the rest of the decade if they did not give way. If he got stuck, they could just leave him there. The three flexed their wings athletically before folding them dragon-like, ready to make the descent down the stone pillars to the display case. Large wings can be a real nuisance when you need to do things indoors.

In the cool gloom below, Penny crouched in the alcove. She felt strangely safe despite the noise from outside and the vibrations she could sense in the stone pillars above her.

Having got their wings under control, the Gargoyles quarrelled over who got to extract the little cat and carry it up to the roof. Dogface was all for tearing it apart on the spot, while the others favoured taking it away along with any other things that they could carry to be examined at their leisure. There had been a mummified foot that looked interesting, insisted Dragonclaw.

It was decided that they should take as many items as could be carried in jaws and claws and return to the roof before taking a closer look. The growling and rumblings went on for some time, interspersed with the occasional lisping from Dragonclaw.

'Dems mummies is mine.'

If it had not been so horrible, it would be quite ridiculous.

Penny could feel the vibrations overhead increase while inside the Mummy case, Indiana Bert, apparently felt nothing. She would have to keep an eye on him, she thought. He has no natural instincts at all. The Gargoyles were coming slowly down the pillars, stone sliding on stone, all one element, alive and moving. Outside, the sounds of applause and the murmurs from the amplified voice droned on in the background.

'AND, NOW OUR FINAL CONTESTANTS OF THE EVENING. PLEASE WELCOME PROFESSOR POPPETT AND POOOOOOODLE.'

There was loud applause as the vibrations from the Gargoyles became more intense. They were not in a hurry, and Penny sensed they were just above her, checking the display case below. The monstrous beasts were slowly coming for the little mummified cat.

Penny tensed and kept her senses alert. She was not quite sure what to do. She was hoping Indiana Bert would leap out of the Mummy case so she could reveal herself once he had seen and chased o the Gargoyles, and that would prove to him that she was innocent. There was only the sound of soft breathing as the dust coated in the fading beams of light. There was a silent moment of tense anticipation.

Suddenly the shriek of a car alarm ripped apart the silence!

Penny knew she must act, and this was the moment. The door to the Mummy case was opening slightly, and the vibration from the pillars above was critical. Penny launched herself into the air and spun around, and faced the oncoming Gargoyles. Her fur stood on end, and her intense blue eyes burned with a cold fire. She snarled and hissed and landed expertly on all four chocolate paws on top of the lower display case, spitting and hissing at the Gargoyles, who stopped suddenly and watched her in amazement. Indiana Bert tumbled out of the Mummy case and gasped at the sight before him.

An angry Siamese cat held back three giant winged Gargoyles by the sheer force of her strong will and indignant rage. Indiana Bert strode forward, and the Gargoyles seemed to melt back into the stone. But this would only last for a few seconds; Penny knew it was time to make for the exit before the Gargoyles decided to grab her. She jumped to the floor and ran fast for the door.

But the Gargoyles were not done with her yet, and Dragonclaw, sliding to the ground, reached out a giant claw, trapping Penny by her slender tail. The delicate chocolate-point tip was being crushed under the pressure. Penny turned and hissed and spat. She knew it was time to get out of there, with or without her tail. She was a terrifying ball of screaming fur.

The car alarm suddenly stopped, and inside and out, all was silent.

Indiana Bert was quick to assess the situation; the little Siamese was innocent, she was protecting the exhibits, and now she was in danger. He stepped forward, unsure of how to move the stone Gargoyle, and so kicked it aggressively, hurting his toe.

Just then, the Museum door swung open and standing framed by the light in the doorway was Gloriana Groom. She has been drawn inside by the commotion and was now frozen to the spot staring at the scene before her. She looked at Penny fighting for her life and at Indiana Bert, kicking the stone shape. Dragonclaw was suddenly very interested in the new, larger shape in the doorway. The other Gargoyles opened their wings and prepared to strike. Ms Groom looked very tasty and was now in their sights.

For the second time, the shriek of a car alarm ripped into the air.

A collective decision was made, and Dragonclaw loosened his grip on Penny's tail to balance himself for a strike at the bigger quarry. In an instant, Penny was gone. She shot past Ms Groom and through the open door. To her right, there were two men with large dogs blocking her way. To her left was the familiar shape of Bruno with his back to her, firmly planted with legs apart, photographing the scene on the lawn. Penny shot between his legs and bounded off to safety.

Meanwhile, time seemed to slow down as the Gargoyles were poised to strike. The alarm was blaring on and on, and Ms Groom was rigid with terror. Indiana Bert was about to have his moment. As the Gargoyles got their wings to full stretch and were moving quickly towards their victim, the world around him went into slow motion. Indiana Bert wished he had said something more heroic, something she would remember. He was about to lose her, and that must not happen. Waving his arms, he screamed,

'NO, YOU FIENDS', above the roar of the alarm. With all his strength, Indiana Bert threw himself ahead of the Gargoyles, knocked Gloriana to the floor, and covered her with his body.

All this was too much like hard work to the Gargoyles, and history had taught them the value of leaving while they still had an advantage. Jostling each other, they shot over the two bodies and through the open door. To their left, there was suddenly a violent flash of light, so extending their wings, they turned and flew over the heads of the two men and their dogs standing to the right, knocking them both to the ground. Then they disappeared into the VIP car park towards the source of the blaring alarm.

There was a terrible, distant crash, and then the car alarm was finally silent.

TWENTY-ONE

On the lawn, the audience held their breath as the Professor gave her hand signal, and Poodle turned to assume the heel position behind her. The Judge gave the command to 'Begin.'

Suddenly the shriek of a car alarm ripped apart the silence!

This irritating piece of modern security has long since become ineffective. It is annoying, and the only person who rushes to the scene is the vehicle owner. The audience murmured their collective irritation but remained in their seats, eyes fixed on the display of canine and owner excellence.

The dogs were agitated, and many panicked. One of the apricot poodles broke free, terrified by the noise and rushed to the catering area to find something edible to quell his fear. Beyond the Quadrangle, a few people stared at the offending vehicle. All were confident the noise would stop soon and would require no action from them.

Poodle completed the turn into the starting position at heel and neatly sat down. The Figure Eight off Lease exercise was about to begin. Two men in the entrance to the marshalling area were watching intently. Why hadn't Poodle rushed around in a panic? What was going wrong? As the Professor inclined her head in a flamenco dancer pose and began to start the figure eight, Poodle, with head erect, showed off the tartan earmuffs.

Both began to move like two stately ships leaving the harbour. The Professor was so engrossed in her performance that her concentration blotted out any sounds or distractions. Poodle, on the other hand, liked to please and simply could not hear anyway; the earmuffs were proving to be very effective.

They reached the mid-point of the figure and paused as the Professor did a series of balletic hand gestures while Poodle watched admiringly before they both continued faultlessly into the second part of the figure.

The audience held their breath at the spectacle before them and hardly noticed that the annoying alarm had suddenly stopped. As they reached the finish, Poodle performed an elegant turn and sat down before both posed in a stance that the Professor had learned from watching Olympic gymnasts.

The audience went mad with delight. Never had such a superlative display of dog handling been seen in all the years of the dog competitions. Never had a pair given such a correct and artistic performance. It was dog and handler in complete harmony.

Wild applause rang out, drowning out the sound of the car alarm, which at that moment started up again. The Dean and Mad Malcolm looked at each other in panic. They had forgotten that the alarm, which once activated, would continue to sound again after a minute's delay.

Both turned quickly and headed back into the

marshalling area to use the remote undetected and silence the noise before they were discovered. Bruno moved forward as they passed by him to get a closer shot of the Professor and Poodle still holding their finishing position while the applause continued.

The alarm continued unheeded, as everyone's attention was on the competitors.

They were a sensation! Mr Thickett was trying not to weep as he noticed the Dutch Barge Dog dig up the far corner of the lawn in its agitation. The camera flashes continued for a minute or so, and no one noticed a small Siamese cat shoot out from between Bruno's extended legs and, in two bounds, leap onto the Judges' Podium.

In her panic to escape, Penny saw her beloved Professor Eagle and ran to him as if her life depended on it, which it did. Two leaps, and then she was on his lap. A surprised Professor Eagle, realising that it was Penny, and that she was trembling in terror, quickly covered her with his academic gown and firmly stroked her shaking body until she relaxed and began to purr.

Professor Poppett broke her pose and, with a happy Poodle trotting by her side, did a lap of victory around the lawn. Bruno suddenly sensed action behind him and turned just in time to see three giant winged creatures burst out from the Museum door. His instincts told him to keep on shooting as they flew outside, knocking over the Dean and Mad Malcolm, who was pointing some device in the direction of the VIP car park. Both were knocked flat on their faces as the Gargoyles rushed over their heads towards the sound of the alarm. The remote was crushed beneath Mad Malcolm as the Fiend and Wrinkles broke loose in a panic and ran towards the lawn to wreak havoc and destruction.

There was a terrible, distant crash, and the alarm finally stopped.

Professor Poppet and Poodle completed their victory lap back on the lawn and made a graceful exit. Fred Planet announced that while the Judges deliberated, the Junior Brass Band would now play *A Life on the Ocean Waves* for their pleasure. No one was quite sure about that. The children thumped out to the centre of the lawn, completely ignoring the Labrador in the muzzle and the funny, wrinkly Pug, who was ripping into the grass. Mishaps were occurring, and attendants with plastic bags and pooper-scoopers were rushing over to clean up the mess and capture the dogs. Mr Thickett was crying pathetically whilst muttering, 'my Precious' under his breath.

On the Judges' podium, the deliberations had begun. Ms Von Katten, the community representative, was a little alarmed by the vibrations coming from Professor Eagle's lap but decided that as he was a literary scholar and happily married man, the sound must be coming from the public address system. The audience was to be saved a second helping of the Junior Brass Band, as there was no doubt about the winners, and the Chair of Judges moved to the microphone to make the announcement and hand out the trophies.

Fred Planet called the audience to attention, and the Band quickly exited to get the best of the cupcakes. Bruno was still dazed by the scene he had just witnessed, but like a true professional, he moved back onto the lawn to photograph the prize-winners.

The Dean and Mad Malcolm reclaimed their misbehaving dogs and stood quietly with heads bowed to await the inevitable judgement. The kind owners comforted the apricot poodles, and all was forgiven. The Dutch Barge Dog was carried to the car and taken home in disgrace.

It was time for the Trophies to be awarded.

TWENTY-TWO

Moments earlier in the Museum doorway, Indiana Bert struggled to his feet and lifted Gloriana in his arms. It was a 'B' movie moment. She was still and silent. He swept aside the equipment on top of the coffin and laid her down gently. All around him, there was noise and commotion and flashes from the photographs. He ignored it all. She was hurt. He smoothed the shiny black hair from her face and leaned over her. 'Kiss of life,' he thought. 'Is she breathing? Oh, my love!'

Gloriana was stunned. He had squashed the air out of her in his attempt to save her from the Gargoyles. Who knows what damage he had done?

'What do I do?' he muttered frantically, and only vaguely recalling his first aid training, he bent over Gloriana and firmly kissed her. Gloriana Groom opened her eyes, and, still confused by the impact, stared at her rescuer.

Dr Eagle saw the hopeless attempt at mouth-to-mouth resuscitation and, realising that an accident had happened, rushed to assist. She was, after all, the only medical person present. Anyone who could handle patients with fangs was quite capable of attending to a human. They were much more manageable. Humans seldom bite your finger off.

'Out of the way, silly man,' she said, brushing Indiana Bert aside as he stood looking down at his fallen angel. Her expert fingers checked the patient and a canine stethoscope listened to her heart.

'Water,' she commanded, and Indiana Bert quickly fetched a cup of water.

Then Gloriana sat up and rested in his strong arms while Dr Eagle asked questions about how many fingers and could she feel her feet. The two lovers just gazed helplessly at each other, and as an attempt to move the patient was not recommended, Dr Eagle instructed her to stay still for a time to ensure an ambulance was not required.

On the lawn, the Trophies were being presented. First, a few minor awards were made, and the delighted winners came forward to shake hands and accept their little cup before being led away by the marshals. Then it was time for the two big awards of the competition. On the Trophy table, the last two big silver cups remained. They were Best in Show, and Best-Groomed Dog and Handler, proudly sponsored by SudsMobile.

'I am delighted to announce,' said Professor Fang, in his best award presenting voice, 'that tonight is unique in the long history of our annual Dog Shows.'

The audience murmured in approval.

'It is quite fitting,' he continued,' that as this is the first time the show has been held in the venerable surroundings of this wonderful University, that the outright winner of both the major trophies should be a member of this famous establishment.'

'I am delighted to announce that the winner of tonight's competition is....

. . .

PROFESSOR POPPETT AND POODLE.'

AND THE AUDIENCE went mad with delight. The Professor, assuming her ballet posture, bowed elaborately, and Poodle did a little bob. Bruno rushed forward to arrange and pose them, and the cameras flashed away to the thunderous applause. The Professor beamed, and Poodle looked very happy too. Storm on the sidelines frantically tweeted to the Professor's followers and posted snaps to Instagram.

The Dean and Mad Malcolm looked very glum. A delighted Ms Gloriana Groom resting on her rescuer's arm was smiling and planning her advertising campaign featuring Poodle wearing the Sponsored by SudsMobile ribbon.

The evening was over. Storm was given vouchers for a free pizza. Bruno was planning to go to his studio to work through the night on the photographs. He was sure he had photographed something extraordinary. Professor Poppett and Poodle were invited to enjoy the board room refreshments with Professor Fang and Ms Von Katten.

Professor Eagle excused himself, and with Penny held close to his chest, went to find his wife. Fred Planet gathered up the distraught Mr Thickett, and having set his staff to the task of clearing up, he steered the poor man to the bar for a restorative beer and pie floater.

Silently, the Dean and Mad Malcolm collected their disgraced pets and forlornly headed to the VIP car park. No words were required. They had played foul and lost, and they knew it. They just hoped that no one else did.

As they exited down the steps to the paved car park

below, they found a group of people, including Bruno, taking photographs of a large, dark car. A BMW. Mad Malcolm's BMW. Some kind of accident people were saying; these old buildings are really not safe. Suppose it fallen on someone. It was shocking. Disgraceful even. People in charge of buildings should be called to account.

The person in charge of buildings was accounting right now. He was counting the cost of repairing his car and how he was going to find a suitable explanation for the insurance company.

Perched squarely in the centre of the crushed roof was Fishbeak. The bonnet was caved in, right in the centre, and Dragonclaw, his wings outstretched, lay across the gouged and scratched paintwork. The passenger side window was smashed, and Dogface had landed on the front seat in a pile of glass. The car was a horrible mess, and no one could explain just how the Gargoyles had fallen from the roof and landed where they did. Freak accident. A good thing no one was hurt. The owner would be very upset. He was. Mad Malcolm collapsed onto the steps and cried on the Dean's shoulder. Their two dogs went to sleep.

Professor and Dr Eagle first made sure that Ms Groom was to be taken home in a taxi by Dr Parker-Betts, who agreed to remain at her side all night if required. Then they walked to the Veterinary School car park, the Professor carrying the sleeping Penny in his arms. When they arrived at the car, he set her down gently on the bonnet and waited until she opened her eyes. Dr Eagle looked her over and concluded that she was unharmed, apart from a shock and a bruised tail. Penny watched them both. She had a terrible fright that evening.

'Well, Penny, it seems you keep getting into trouble, and we think that it is not safe for you to live in the University anymore. So,' she continued while her husband gently opened the rear door, 'you must decide if you would like a little holiday with us; not forever, of course, just for now.'

There was a long pause as they both looked at her kindly and waited.

Penny thought that it would be okay, for now, of course, but not forever. She studied them both with her intense and rather sleepy blue eyes and decided she could trust them. Then she jumped into the back seat and went peacefully to sleep.

The Eagles smiled. They were going to be very, very happy.

TWENTY-THREE

Over the next few days, the University lapsed back into being a quiet backwater in a city of high energy and urgency. When Mad Malcolm arrived the following day to face the dreadful ruin of his car and organise a tow truck, he was surprised to find the Gargoyles had gone. There was just a big pile of glass and some huge dents left as evidence. He assumed that someone had moved them, although he was at a loss to explain how they got there in the first place.

Both he and the Dean had been mysteriously knocked to the ground by something flying overhead. But Gargoyles? Not possible. He looked up and was pretty sure that none of the stone beasts were missing from the roof edges. There were so many that it was hard to tell if they had fallen down. His hatred of Gothic architecture increased.

He did feel a little relieved as he rang his insurance company and said it was vandalism, over-enthusiastic students. He was sure of it. Whether the three Gargoyles could be called vandals was unclear, but it would do. Plenty of people had seen them on the wreck of the car, but in the absence of no actual concrete evidence, the incident had not taken place. A sort of group amnesia was setting in fast.

Gloriana Groom and Indiana Bert were pretty clear about the Gargoyles. They had seen them. However, the horror of the Gargoyle attack was fading slowly, as it was the reason that the lovers were now holding hands and walking along the beach discussing their future together. Gloriana shared her great love of cats, and Indiana Bert said that his mother's house was full of them, so he was sure his mother would love her too. Marriage was on both their minds. They left a line of footprints in the wet sand as they walked off to a happy life together.

Penny was given a bath and some flea drops. Then she was brushed, cuddled, and given some special healthy food and was allowed to sleep on the Eagles' bed. If we peer through the big windows of the Eyrie, we will see two pairs of feet entwined under the duvet, and a content Siamese cat curled up between them.

Bruno worked through the night and all the next day. He was wild with excitement. Some of the photographs were astonishing. As he reviewed the images in order, he recalled the moment he was shooting Professor Poppet and Poodle's amazing performance. The awful car alarm blaring on and on and two contestants continuing as if nothing was happening; an expression of deep contentment on the Professor's face and Poodle's perky ears draped over the tartan ear muffs, which blotted out the sound.

At that moment, he had suddenly been aware that Penny had shot between his legs and bounded off towards the Judges' podium. As she disappeared, he had instinctively swung around and started shooting in the direction that Penny had run from. The resulting images were beyond belief. The first two images were of giant winged beasts flying towards him. Bruno poured himself a strong drink. Each one was slightly different, but all had a wingspan as enormous as an eagle.

'Are these things real?' he asked himself.

In the subsequent shots, the three creatures had turned and were flying away from him, alarmed, he thought, by the flash from his camera. In the next photo, the three monsters were flying over the heads of two male contestants with their dogs. In the next shot, the two men were thrown to the ground, and their dogs had run in terror.

The final shot of the sequence showed the three beasts flying away from him and disappearing out of shot towards the source of the persistent car alarm.

Bruno had a strong coffee to bring himself back to reality, and then he studied the photographs taken a short time later in the car park. The three creatures, and now he could see they were Gargoyles, were lying as still as stone on the wreck of an almost new BMW. How they had got there was not clear, but Bruno had seen them flying with his own eyes, and if they were playing tricks on him, then the photographs were definitely not.

He had many pictures of the car, and the crowd gathered around. He also had a splendid shot of the owner of the car sobbing pathetically on the shoulder of a man in an embroidered baseball jacket. Their dogs were lying at their feet, exhausted by the whole thing. A good pose, he thought. These later photographs were processed quickly. He felt given the number of amateur photos taken, he should dispatch some images of the car wreck to the local news outlets without delay.

It was the photographs of the flying Gargoyles that would require further and more considered thought. These were the money shots. They were also a little hard to believe, and as he was not someone who wished to be accused of faking his work, this had to be handled carefully.

He had many delightful photographs of Professor Poppet and Poodle performing and winning the competition. Bruno selected the best and dispatched copies via his agent to Celebrity Dog, the local newspapers and the event organisers. He then printed out the best and arranged for a courier to deliver them to the Professor's office. He also prepared one particular photograph in a sealed packet marked; For Storm's Eyes Only. He thought she should share his astounding discovery, as he knew she would be interested and amazed. He also had an idea that Penny may have escaped from those horrible jaws and claws, and he was very glad.

After long contemplation, he got on the phone to his agent, suggesting she might contact Scientific American Magazine, World Photography Awards and the Journal of Scientific Exploration. He asked her to find some scientific experts to comment on the photographs. He wisely added his copyright information as a watermark on each image and added the date stamp. He had an idea that these photographs might cause a sensation. He might be able to buy himself something nice and red and fast with the expected financial returns. He booked an appointment with his hairdresser as he expected to be interviewed.

Storm arrived on Monday morning, a little worst for the pizza. She had many packages to look at before the Professor had her racing about for the day. The first packages were a special delivery from Bruno. She opened the large package for the Professor and, after a glance at the beautiful photographs, knocked at the Professor's door to deliver them.

Storm had never heard the Professor squeal in delight,

but she did today. The photos were spread out on a low table so Poodle could inspect them as well. Both dog and owner were delighted and beamed with joy. Storm turned to go and was called back by the Professor, who handed her a small box. This was a real surprise.

'From Poodle,' said Professor Poppett, and Beloved Poodle licked Storm's leg instead of a kiss.

Storm thanked them both and returned to her own office. She now had three small boxes and one large envelope to open. As the Professor had no immediate racing around for her to do, she opened the first box, the one from the Professor. It contained a silver poodle brooch, just like the real Poodle. Storm was thrilled and pinned it on her jacket.

Next, there was a package from the Eagles. There was a hand-written note.

To Storm, with grateful thanks for bringing Penny into our lives. She will be loved and treasured. We hope you will visit often.

Storm opened the box and found another silver brooch of a Siamese cat, looking just like Penny. This was truly wonderful. She pinned it next to her Poodle brooch.

The final parcels were from Bruno. She opened the envelope marked For Storm's Eyes Only, and stared at the photograph in disbelief. A vast creature with giant wings and claws was flying straight towards the camera. It was huge and terrifying. It was unbelievable. If this monster had been chasing Penny, it was a good thing that she was now safe with the Eagles. Storm locked the photograph in the desk drawer.

The second parcel was a small box. Inside was a third silver brooch. This time it was a winged creature looking very much like the ones in the photo. Storm pinned it on her jacket. The three silver brooches looked very nice together. There was a note, too.

To Storm, who makes all things possible. From your friend, Bruno.

Storm had tears in her eyes as she sat down at her desk to write her 'thank you' notes.

The End

DEAR READER

Thank you for reading my book. You had so many choices and you chose me. I appreciate it. Writing can be a lonely career, so I would be grateful if you could leave a review - just a few stars will do nicely. If you enjoyed my book, please tell your friends and family. Positive word-of-mouth recommendations helps me find new readers and write more books.

Sign up for my monthly Newsletter and download a free short story. I promise not to overwhelm you with emails or spam. That way, you will be the first to know when there is a new book for you to enjoy.

1. The University Cat: A Tale for Grown-Ups & Graduates

2. Beware the Cat : The Shakespearean Chronicles

3. The Reluctant Gift

4. The Greening of Ginger George

Tails from the Cat Shop: The Kitten's Story - CyberCat Series Prequel

Sign up for the latest updates and news

https://jansayer.com

Enter the world of the **CyberCat Series**, and meet Penny, a one-of-a-kind Siamese Cat with an independent streak, nine mythical lives, and the right amount of attitude to keep things interesting. Follow her as she navigates diverse worlds and ages, extending a helpful chocolate-coloured paw and leaving an indelible mark on the hearts of those she meets.

Fun and fright in the Gothic splendour a university in Sydney. **The University Cat: A Tale for Grown-Ups and Graduates** comes alive when an exuberant poodle puppy leaps over the writer's desk, igniting a thrilling escapade celebrating the quirks of some remarkable academics and friends in Australia.

The CyberCat finds herself in Shakespeare's London and meets the man himself. The delightful chaos of **Beware the Cat: The Shakespearean Chronicles** is inspired by a fascinating piece of early English literature, combining historical intrigue with contemporary wit. Populated with historic characters and a mischievous feline who has slipped through time, it weaves a tale of an exhilarating yet perilous age.

The Reluctant Gift launches Penny, the CyberCat, into another enthralling adventure, this time captivating the crowds as she becomes an exhibit in Victorian London's most spectacular showcase; the Great Exhibition of 1851. As Penny navigates this perplexing world, she becomes entangled in a high-stakes adventure to prevent the theft of a priceless brooch.

In **The Greening of Ginger George,** Penny returns to her comfortable home in Australia, but a violent storm and a strange new kitten disrupt her life. Penny joins the fight against unscrupulous developers who want to turn the forest into a spa for rich tourists.

Explore the series' origins with **Tails from the Cat Shop: The Kitten's Story**, a prequel set in a virtual world that blurs the lines between reality and imagination.

Jessika Jenvieve is the pen name of crime writer, Jan Sayer.

For more in the CyberCat Series, sign up for my mailing list: https://www.jansayer.com/

www.ingramcontent.com/pod-product-compliance
Lightning Source LLC
Chambersburg PA
CBHW031417150726
47989CB00002B/688